HARLEQUIN®
Presents

Harlequin Presents never fails to bring you the most
gorgeous, brooding alpha heroes—so don't miss out on
this month's irresistible collection!

When handsome Peter Ramsey discovers Erin's having
his baby in *The Billionaire's Captive Bride* by
Emma Darcy, he offers her the only thing he can
think of to guarantee his child's security—marriage! In
The Greek Tycoon's Unwilling Wife by Kate Walker,
Andreas has lost his memory, but what will happen
when he recalls throwing Rebecca out of his house on
their wedding day—for reasons only he knows? If you're
feeling festive, you'll love *The Boss's Christmas Baby*
by Trish Morey, where a boss discovers his convenient
mistress is expecting his baby. In *The Spanish Duke's
Vigin Bride* by Chantelle Shaw, ruthless Spanish
billionaire Duke Javier Herrera sees in Grace an
opportunity for revenge *and* a contract wife! In
The Italian's Pregnant Mistress by Cathy Williams,
millionaire Angelo Falcone has Francesca in his power
and in his bed, and this time he won't let her go. In
Contracted: A Wife for the Bedroom by Carol Marinelli,
Lily knows Hunter's ring will only be on her finger
for twelve months, but soon a year doesn't seem long
enough! Finally, brand-new author Susanne James brings
you *Jed Hunter's Reluctant Bride*, where Jed demands
Cryssie marry him because it makes good business sense,
but Cryssie's feelings run deeper.... Enjoy!

Elizabeth Power
RUTHLESS REUNION

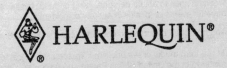

TORONTO • NEW YORK • LONDON
AMSTERDAM • PARIS • SYDNEY • HAMBURG
STOCKHOLM • ATHENS • TOKYO • MILAN • MADRID
PRAGUE • WARSAW • BUDAPEST • AUCKLAND

ISBN-13: 978-0-373-18881-9
ISBN-10:   0-373-18881-1

RUTHLESS REUNION

First North American Publication 2007.

www.eHarlequin.com

Printed in U.S.A.

All about the author...
Elizabeth Power

ELIZABETH POWER was born in Bristol, where she still lives with her husband in a three hundred-year-old cottage. A keen reader, as a teenager she had already made up her mind to be a novelist. But it wasn't until a few weeks before her thirtieth birthday, when Elizabeth was thinking about what she had done with her first thirty years and realized she had been telling herself she would "start writing tomorrow" for at least twelve of them, that she took up writing seriously. A short time later, the letter that was to change her life arrived from Harlequin. *Rude Awakening* was to be published in 1986. After a prolonged absence, Elizabeth is pleased to be back at her keyboard, with new romances already in the works.

Of her writing, Elizabeth says emotional intensity is paramount in her books. She says, "times, places and trends change, but emotion is timeless." A powerful story line with maximum emotion, set in a location in which you can really live and breathe while the story unfolds, is what she strives for. Good food and wine come high on her list of priorities, and what better way to sample these delights than by just having to take another trip to some new exotic resort. Oh, and of course, to find a location for the next book!

For Alan and the Bermudian Longtail.

CHAPTER ONE

IT WAS the face behind the camera that intrigued him most.

In all the years he had been coming to Bermuda Alex had never seen anyone quite like her, and with all the problems he had left back in England—the responsibilities of a family fortune, discrepancies in investments, Luke's death—his spring break here this year had scarcely appealed. Until now.

The young woman, however, was still intent on capturing the magnificent splendour of the ice sculpture standing near the far wall of the hotel ballroom behind him, and Alex took the opportunity to let his gaze wander, unashamedly and unnoticed, over the rest of this equally magnificent creature.

Tall, slim, in her very early twenties, she was one of the few females at the party tonight not wearing black, which marked her as independent-minded and free-spirited to his way of thinking. The heavy weight of her sleek dark hair—every bit as black as his own—was a striking contrast to the cream chiffon-fine dress that moved fluidly against her body, the long transparent sleeves somehow lending added sensuality to a bodice cut so low he could see where the deep cleavage of her generous breasts ended and the pale flesh of her midriff began.

As his eyes lingered on those full rounded breasts, a hard, basic urge ripped through him, stronger than any he had known in his life.

Reluctantly he forced his gaze down, noticing how the dress hugged her small waist and her smooth hips to whisper around her in a series of concealed splits, so that the barest movement revealed tantalising glimpses of her creamy thighs. The tapered hemline of the dress caressed long legs that finished in fine-strapped silver sandals, the height of the stilettos enhancing already shapely calves and ankles.

Self-assured. Poised. A woman who didn't mind being noticed. Or one, he thought suddenly—conversely—with his keen, trained mind kicking into gear, who needed to advertise her confidence in order to conceal a distinct lack of any.

But her camera had come to rest on him.

As the sudden flash captured the hard, questioning angles of his face, he saw her mouth open, as though her own audacity had surprised her. Her mouth, like her toes and the scarlet-tipped fingers still holding the small device, was creamy red, a full, sultry mouth that he had the sudden hot and almost unbearable urge to plunder.

Slowly then, she lowered the camera, and Alex felt as if his breath was being dragged through his lungs when he saw that her face matched everything her body promised.

It was the face of an angel—and a siren. Her skin resembled porcelain against the deep sheen of her hair. Her eyebrows were finely arched, her lashes long and dark over seductively slanting eyes.

The sounds of the party going on around him seemed—like the chatting, laughing faces that filled the hotel's glittering ballroom—superimposed on his brain. For him there was no one else in the room but this sensuous, unsmiling beauty. Nor did he want there to be. He wanted them all to disappear so that he could walk over to her unhampered, get her to acknowledge him—accept him—and do what his primal instincts were urging him to do. Possess her utterly and completely.

He dipped his head in the subtlest acknowledgement. She didn't turn away, just stood there, as though hypnotised by the same powerful force that held him in thrall. But neither did she smile, and suddenly, in those strikingly amber eyes of hers and through his own private turmoil, he recognised misery of the most devastating kind.

Curiosity, on top of everything else, would have had him abandoning his companions to close the gap between him and this beautiful girl. But then the youth standing next to her touched her arm to gain her attention and she turned abruptly away.

She didn't want to be here. She hadn't wanted to come.

After the trauma of the past five weeks Sanchia Stevens couldn't understand how she had allowed herself to be talked into attending a party to celebrate the expansion of one of the island's largest hotels—except that Francine and Rick had insisted upon it, had said that it would do her good. But Rick and Francine had already left, under the pretext, she was sure, of Francine having a headache, and she guessed that they thought she had 'fixed herself up' with the sycophantic young man who seemed determined to cling to her and had decided to leave her to it.

They didn't know that she had declined to go with them because she hadn't wanted to go back to the hotel, didn't want to be alone—because that meant thinking, and she didn't want to have to think. Nor did they know that this was supposed to have been her honeymoon. They had naturally assumed she had come on holiday alone, simply looking for a good time, which was why they had been so ready to abandon her. But that had been nearly an hour ago, just as she'd been taking pictures of that swan sculpted out of ice, and the man she had been reckless enough to capture with her camera hadn't taken his eyes off her since.

His black wavy hair, brushed straight back, was impeccably groomed, like the rest of him, although the immaculate tailoring of his dark suit, white shirt and tie did very little to tame the contours of a body that was honed to disciplined fitness: lean, broad-shouldered, intensely male.

Sitting on one of the high stools that flanked the bar, she could see him still, across the heads of several other guests, talking with the same group of people he had been talking to all night. Serious-minded, important-looking people, from the intensity of their conversation. Dignitaries or government officials? Sanchia speculated, and recognised one from a picture she'd seen hanging in the vestibule as the owner of the hotel. However, where dominance and sheer physical presence played a part, the man who was interesting her most outstripped them all.

His features were strikingly etched, uncompromisingly handsome beneath the rich bronze of a Bermuda tan. But it was that air of authority that drew her eyes unwittingly to him as much as to those darkly aloof features. Instinctively, she knew he would be a formidable opponent, would command respect and inspire awe in whatever game he chose to play.

And he had chosen to play for her.

A little shudder ran through her at that inexplicable acknowledgement, immediately followed by a leap of hard excitement when she saw that his company was now dispersing and he was already striding over to the bar.

'Hello, I'm Alex.' His voice was chocolate-rich and deep, that air of authority coupled with the impact of a devastating sexual charisma now that he was up close, making her put her reluctant fingers into the firm, warm clasp of his. 'And you are?'

Her temperature sky-rocketing, she lifted heavy eyes to a pair that were a steel-hard, penetrating grey. 'Wishing you'd let go of my hand.'

He didn't immediately, retaining it just long enough for her to recognise the power of an intrepid will. Through her silent wretchedness a little voice warned her to be careful.

'Could I get you another drink?'

'Very probably,' she murmured, her claws unsheathed by the pain of bitter betrayal, making him a scapegoat for all his sex. 'I'd imagine there's very little you couldn't do,' she added levelly, looking him up and down in a way designed to faze him but which only resulted in producing a throb of something elemental in her that was almost frightening in its intensity.

'Then I'll rephrase that.' He slipped a hand into his trouser pocket, and amended with emphasis, '*May* I get you a drink?' From his perfect diction it was clear he was neither Bermudian or American, but full-blooded English. From the hint of impatience in that deep voice, it was also obvious he didn't usually have to work this hard.

'Better.' Her sultry mouth curved in the merest smile as she picked up the Martini glass from the bar, put it to her lips. 'But the answer's still thanks, but no thanks.'

'Too complicated?'

'Much too complicated,' she responded, noticing now the fine lines around his eyes and the grooves etching his mouth, as though he had been driving himself too hard, or been under some strain.

'Really? I was under the impression you wanted me to come over and speak to you.'

'Were you?' She gave a brittle little laugh, unintentionally tantalising, provocative, and saw the glint of something dark and dangerous leap in his eyes. Setting her glass back down on the bar, she glanced away, feigning interest in some laughter coming from one of the tables before enquiring casually, 'Are you married?' Not that it mattered, she assured herself firmly. He was much too sophisticated and dangerous for her to be playing with.

'Married?' He made it sound as though she had insulted him even by suggesting it. 'No, I'm not married.'

Perhaps she had insulted him, she thought, some sixth sense telling her he wasn't the type of man to approach a woman if he had a wife somewhere. A man with ethics. Uncommitted. In control. A man who could make her forget...

Sanchia shook the shocking, disturbing notion away, wondering where it had come from.

'What's your name?'

Above the soft music drifting out from behind the bar, the equally soft command stirred a contrary desire in her to rebel—against him, against the effect he was having on her, against herself. 'Is that a prerequisite?'

Something like annoyance flashed in his eyes but was quickly erased. 'A prerequisite for what?'

A rather sensual smile played around his mouth now and, held by the snare of his flagrant masculinity, Sanchia's gaze faltered, her brain acknowledging the power of mind and body that lay behind that impeccable façade. He would know how to please, pleasure, protect a woman—for as long as she was his at any rate, she fantasised, shaken by her own wild speculation. He could also hurt her, if she played this dangerous game with him. But maybe that was what she wanted, she thought suddenly—crazily. The diversion this man could provide would numb the pain.

She had had more to drink than was wise if she was thinking like that. Not that she'd really had very much, and not so much that the man standing beside her would have noticed, but certainly one or two glasses more than she was accustomed to.

Her sparkling eyes turned the deepest amber as she looked up into his face. A hard, handsome face, whose forcefulness filled her with such a contrary mixture of rebellion and excitement that she wanted to challenge it and lose herself to it all at the same time.

She gave a heedless shrug. 'Whatever,' she answered, with another fleeting little smile, and felt his gaze burn over her shoulders and her generous breasts in tacit acknowledgement. A reckless heat licked through her, and deep inside her something throbbed in startling response. 'Isn't it all part of the game?'

'The game?'

'You ask my name. You buy me a drink. We wind up in bed. Isn't that the natural progression of things?'

'You're very direct.'

You'd be direct, her mind screamed, *if your fiancé had just killed himself and the other woman he'd been shacking up with!*

'Is there any other way to be?' Her dark lashes swept downwards, camouflaging agony. 'Why cloak it behind a charade of needless civilities?'

'Why, indeed?'

She could sense that he didn't mean that. He was just a little bit shocked by her plain speaking, she suspected, although he wasn't allowing it to show.

'And have you always been so cynical?' he went on.

A smile curved the corners of his mouth again, a hard, sexy mouth that in another situation would show a woman heaven. She wondered what it would be like to feel its demanding pressure on hers.

'Cynical?' Her slanting eyes made an unconscious survey of his magnificent physical attributes. Broad shoulders made sleek by exclusive tailoring. A solid walled chest, tight waist and hard, lean hips. 'I'm sorry.' Her smile was provocative, blazing from bright lips that were struggling to conceal pure pain. 'I didn't mean to be.'

'Didn't you?' Those grey eyes smiled, but there was a mild reprimand in the deep timbre of his voice.

He was using his gaze like dangerous visual foreplay—and it was working! She had never felt so aroused in her life. Those stimulating eyes had marked her out for his possession, and, much as she wanted to resist their lethally hypnotic power, she didn't seem to have any defence against it. All night long there had been a silent exchange of something flagrantly sexual between them, a dark and mutually carnal demand that was screaming out to be met. She didn't know how she could feel such a barrage of conflicting emotions. Excitement slashing through grief. Desire riding side by side with pain. The weight of it was almost unbearable.

'So you prefer anonymity?' That masculine voice throbbed with sensual amusement, and yet suddenly she recognised some raw and personal anguish behind the formidable strength in that face. 'Most intriguing.'

'Why not?' Her fingers curled painfully into her palms from the urge to reach up and touch him, touch the elemental heart of whatever was causing him to suffer. 'We aren't going to see each other again.'

'Aren't we?'

The determination in those two words sent a little frisson through her. She wanted to challenge them—challenge that glaring authority—but words wouldn't come.

'Well, now that's settled, let me tell you what I—'

She wasn't aware of lifting her fingers to that firm, communicative mouth, only of its sensual warmth beneath their gentle pressure to silence him.

For a fleeting moment she stared at him, shocked by her own temerity. Mouth parched, breath coming quickly, blood pumping through every stimulated vessel, her hungry amber eyes were drowning in the incandescent heat of smouldering grey.

She had crossed a line, she realised hectically—stupidly! And if she stayed there would be no turning back.

Grabbing her camera off the bar, she jumped off the stool and, without a word, twisted away from him, out of the ballroom into the quiet lobby and into the haven of a waiting lift.

Slipping her camera strap over her shoulder, she stood breathless, trembling, wanting only for the lift to swallow her, when an impeccably sleeved arm sliced between the closing doors.

They yielded, allowing her pursuer entry, and whirred shut again, locking them both in a bubble of screaming intimacy that was swelling with each straining second.

They stared at each other like combatants, chests heaving, mouths turning almost savage.

There's no way out, Sanchia thought, and felt the white-hot tide of desire pool in a molten heat in her loins.

And then the bubble burst and he was dragging her against him. Or had she reached for him first? She wasn't sure. Only that that savage mouth was devouring her, just as hers was devouring him, responding to the fierce heat of his demands with throbbing, driving needs of her own.

His hands were twisting in the gleaming swathe of her hair with an almost painful pleasure, while hers revelled in the thick dark strength of his even as she sagged against him, weakened and clinging to him for support. Hungrily, she brought her fingers clawing down over his face, over the hard, exciting texture of his cheek and jaw, sinking her nails into his broad shoulders with a little cry of pleasure when one arm moved to catch her hard against his powerfully aroused body.

Her breasts ached for his hands, craving their warmth against their full, aching sensitivity, and like an extension of her own thinking he seemed to know. She felt the moist heat at the very heart of her as his hand slid easily inside her dress, the hard contraction of her body's crying out to have this man possess her, to lose her pain and misery in the torturous rapture he could provide.

The whirr of the lift moving upwards was drowned by their laboured breathing. It whined to a halt, opening into a private corridor. A route merely to the penthouse suite.

It registered with Sanchia only numbly as the man lifted his head, his features flushed from the hunger that rode him—rode them both. She hadn't even been aware of him pressing the indicator button.

There was no one about. Only the two of them and the thick silence that came with the luxury he had paid for.

He was waiting. Giving her a choice, she realised in that split moment of breathless silence. *Go or stay.*

Something urged her to pull free from this reckless path she seemed to have carved out for herself. But she knew she had relinquished all choice downstairs in the bar.

She wasn't aware of actually walking to his door, or of his using a card-key to open it. She was only aware, as his arms came round her again, that she had invited this, and that she couldn't prevent what was going to happen any more than she could stop the boilers breaking over the reef beyond the coral-crushed beaches of the South Shore.

Their mouths melded, hot and hungrily—even before he had slammed the door behind them—in desperate imitation of the act that was to follow.

It was an act that Alex knew he couldn't have denied himself even if he had wanted to.

He was using her—heaven help him! Using her to rid himself of the demons that were plaguing him. In the same way, he strongly suspected, that she was using him.

But for all that he couldn't get enough of her. Of her sweet moist mouth, her perfume, the earth-shattering promise of her body. He couldn't get enough of her, and to relieve himself of the deep ache of wanting he lifted her up, so that he could feel her luscious legs as well as her arms around him, his mouth plundering hers as he moved urgently through with her into his bedroom.

I can't get enough of him! Sanchia thought, burning for him, inhaling the scent of his aftershave as though it was vital oxygen, excited by his strength, unbearably aroused by the grazing texture of that impeccable suit against the soft flesh of her inner thighs.

His suite was in darkness, though French doors stood open to the scents and sounds that filled the bedroom from a private roof garden, and the whistling of frogs and lizards in the softly illuminated foliage was a sensuous song that heightened the eroticism of the warm Bermudian night.

The big bed yielded beneath them as they toppled down onto it together.

I want you! she thought, glorying in his actions as he pushed back the flimsy barrier that separated her from him and claimed her full, responsive breasts as his own.

She gave a small strangled cry, her breath shuddering through her from the ecstasy of those marauding hands, the sudden heat of his mouth on one swollen tip bringing her straining towards him in a wild frenzy of need.

Oh, *please*…! She didn't want to wait, couldn't wait. She wanted him *now!*

Alex groaned from the heat of desire that was throbbing through his body. He had never felt so out of control in his life.

He was far too hot—too hard, he realised, mentally flaying himself for getting himself into this situation, wondering how, if he let things run their natural course, he was ever going to last. He couldn't even protect her—or himself. Gone were the days when he'd gone out equipped with a young stag's hope of getting lucky. He was thirty-six years old. A leading barrister, for goodness' sake! With responsibilities, common sense… Except that it seemed to have deserted him in his need for this girl.

He knew he should love her as she should be loved. With care and consideration, after a quiet, romantic evening, with all the skill and mastery of a long-perfected technique. Not like this, like some callow youth…

He hesitated for the briefest moment, dragged back from the edge of a precipice from which there could be no return. But then she arched her back and her writhing hips collided sensuously with his, shaking his very foundations from beneath him, and in that moment he knew he was finished.

He was doing this, Sanchia thought, as though he was seeking respite from something. She guessed that he wasn't usually so rough or possessive as he caught her wrists above her head and ground his lower body against hers in hard domination, but whatever unknown entity was driving him, she didn't want to know or care. He was dark and dangerous, and she needed the excitement he offered to obliterate her savage misery.

He made little work of dispensing with her white lacy string, his hands hard and uncompromising, but when his fingers slid into her softness, checking her readiness to receive him, they were unexpectedly gentle.

She whimpered her need, her body contracting around his fingers in a way that made Alex groan with frustration. He heard her moan softly in protest as he withdrew them, clenching his teeth in throbbing anticipation as he moved, adjusting his position before plunging into her, hard and deep.

She uttered a deeply choked sound that was lost beneath the chorus of the night creatures in the luxuriant foliage, and started to climax immediately, each deepening thrust of his body bringing her bucking and sobbing beneath him through the agonising ecstasy of his own release.

When Sanchia started to think again, she couldn't believe what she had allowed to happen.

Why had she done it? she berated herself mercilessly. She had never been so stupidly reckless in her life!

She groaned a protest under his pinioning weight, so that he moved away from her immediately.

She couldn't look at him as she readjusted her dress over her virtual nakedness, then groped for her errant string on the crumpled bedspread.

'Are you looking for this?' He was on his feet on the other side of the bed, amazingly in control again. Not as she felt. Shocked by her actions. Cheapened by them. Ashamed.

She grabbed the scrap of lace from his tanned hand, unable to meet his eyes.

Dear heaven! He hadn't even undressed! Such had been their urgency for each other. Grief and betrayal had driven her into his arms, she realised bitterly, but it had been a purely animal coupling, nothing more.

Now pangs of self-disgust, and one Martini too many after days of too little food, had her rolling off the bed and stumbling instinctively towards his bathroom, where she was physically sick.

What type of man took a woman without any preliminaries, she wondered, groping for a towel. Just out of pure need to sate his lust? But she knew she had been a willing participant, and she had shrugged off his attempt at those preliminaries, craving only the oblivion from her screaming emotions that she knew she would find in his arms. So what type of woman did that make her?

'Are you all right?'

Her eyes hurt from the light he had snapped on.

She didn't look at him, grateful for the hair that fell forward, hiding the mess of her make-up and her blotchy face as she wiped her mouth on a towel that smelled too keenly of his aftershave lotion. 'Fine.' It came out flat and muffled.

'I hadn't realised you'd had that much to drink. I thought you were in total control of what you were doing. I'd never have brought you up here if I had.'

He was blaming himself. That deep note of remorse in his voice told her all too chillingly that he didn't normally give in to his animal urges with such basic disregard. And now he regretted it.

'Don't feel too bad about it.' Unable to unload what had driven her to behave in a way that was grossly out of character with this total stranger—because he *was* still a stranger, for all the intimacy they had just shared—she didn't even bother to explain that she hadn't been drinking to excess, that she wasn't proud—any more than he was—of what she had allowed to happen. He must think her a promiscuous, half-inebriated fool, and the quicker she got away from him, the better.

Matter-of-factly, he said, 'It shouldn't have happened like that.'

'No.'

'I should have put you in a cab and sent you home.'

She looked at him squarely at last, her stomach turning over even now from the impact of his devastating looks, that mouth that had kissed her senseless, his dominating, hard-edged masculinity.

'Yes.' What had she imagined? she wondered, feeling the pangs of a wounded injustice that seemed to anaesthetise all her other emotions. That a man like him would have wanted her in any other way than for her body?

'I'll get you some coffee,' he said.

When he came back a few minutes later to check up on how she was, the bedroom was deserted. So was the bathroom, and the light that was still on illuminated his way as he strode purposefully back into the sitting room.

The door to the suite was ajar, he noticed, and quickly stepped out into the quiet corridor. The lift was in use, the illuminated buttons indicating its occupation, its movement on a lower level of the hotel.

It could be her, he realised, knowing he stood a cat in hell's chance of catching her. Brow furrowing, his attention slid automatically to the Emergency Exit door at the end of the corridor, just past his own.

Something other than his five basic senses drew him towards it. The night-scented air greeted him with a rush of humid warmth as he pushed it open, bringing with it the continuous whistling of lizards and the restless surge of the sea.

He saw her then, some way off in the distance—a shadowy figure, illuminated by the beach lamps, sandals hanging from her fingers, racing away over the soft pink sand.

She had been so keen to get away from him she hadn't waited for the lift. She had used the fire escape instead.

Inside, Alex felt numb. He knew he'd never catch her. She'd be lost to him even if he sprang after her now, jumped the steps below him two by two.

She had come to his bed and then left, unable, he felt sure, to face him. To face anyone, he suspected now. Which could be another explanation for her not using the lift.

But she could be carrying his child…

The thought jolted him like a whiplash and he cursed himself for his irresponsibility, for letting his raging hormones rule him instead of his head. It wasn't a foregone conclusion that she was taking the Pill.

He wanted to yell after her. To stop her in her tracks. To drag her back—at least until he knew one way or the other. But a group of guests had wandered out onto the restaurant terrace way below. He could hear the muted strains of their conversation, their oblivious laughter, and as he watched the girl being swallowed up by the shadows of the Bermudian night he realised for the first time, and with another, much more shocking jolt, that he didn't even know her name.

CHAPTER TWO

THE jury were being sworn in.

When her turn came Sanchia knew she would have to stand up, and a small dart of panic shot through her.

It wasn't enough that the courtroom, with its high arched windows and dark paneling, was oppressive. Or that she could sense the eyes of the awesome-looking defence barrister who was standing nearest the jury box boring into her in a way that was making her feel decidedly self-conscious. No, it was the unsettling feeling on top of all that that she had done something similar before; there was some weird *déjà vu* in sitting here among the sculpted halls and corridors of this majestic building that was sending spears of pain across her temples, making her palms hot and clammy.

Perhaps she should have claimed exemption when she had been summoned here today. But, having been selected at random under English law, she had wanted to do her duty like any upstanding citizen, believing that she was well enough, keen to start functioning normally again. Putting her few photographic jobs on hold to take two weeks' compulsory jury service was just another stepping stone towards that normality—another small opportunity to pick up the tenuous threads of her life.

The court official thrust the book towards her as she got shakily to her feet. On top was a card containing the words she had to say.

'Just a moment, m'lud.' The deep commanding voice of the defence barrister threatened to rock her off balance as it brought the swearing-in process to an abrupt halt. The panelled walls seemed to throb in the silence that followed. The official made a silencing gesture to Sanchia, who could only stand and stare at the man who had halted the proceedings.

Although it was the judge he was addressing, those grey eyes hadn't lifted from hers. Sharp, penetrating eyes that would miss nothing, and which marked a calculating intelligence and a keen mind.

In the dark robes of his profession he had a formidable presence, from his commanding height, olive skin and sleek black hair—visible beneath the compulsory wig—to the black winged brows above those intelligent eyes and the dark shading of his jaw, which only served to strengthen an already flagrant masculinity.

'I'm afraid I have to challenge this juror.'

All eyes were turned towards Sanchia. Hers, though, were still trapped by the power of the man who seemed to dominate the court.

With a crushing sense of foreboding she was struck by the ominous notion that somewhere in another lifetime she had been tried and judged and sentenced by this man. Perspiration beaded her forehead, made her neck feel sticky beneath the neat French pleat and the collar of her pale green jacket, and her head started to throb.

'I would ask that this juror be removed.'

On his deep-voiced instruction, that was more a command than a request, Sanchia thought her legs were going to buckle under her.

Her face pale against the dark twist of her hair, Sanchia's eyes questioned his in bewildered challenge. But he didn't relent—just stood there staring at her, as though he had seen some sort of ghost. And as the court official ushered her away she felt that grey gaze following her until she had left the court, and it was then that her legs finally gave out.

Alex was immensely relieved that he had managed to get a brief but immediate adjournment. All he had wanted to do after he had seen Sanchia walk into that court—heard her name called out so that he had been forced to challenge it and have her removed—was race after her, stop her from leaving the building no matter what it took.

He needed answers to so many questions. Like where had she gone when she had run out on him that day? And what had she been doing for the past two years? Where was she living? And why, when she had first seen him in that courtroom, had she not spoken up and excused herself, as the law required any juror sitting on a case to do if they recognised someone directly involved with it. She had glanced towards him several times, been fully aware that he was there. Perhaps, he speculated, his thoughts whirring round his cool, normally ordered brain, she had been too embarrassed to say anything. Had hoped, through some small miracle, that she'd get away with it. He gritted his teeth against the familiar kick in his loins just from remembering the way she had fixed him with those cool, seductively slanting amber eyes.

Perhaps she had been planning just to sit there and enjoy watching him fazed, he thought, his jaw clenching at the gut-wrenching possibility. She had to know that her presence would have rocked the ground on which he stood. And yet, he thought, puzzled, as his robe billowed behind him in his swift, determined passage to the room where he had instructed one of the ushers to detain her, from that almost intimidated look in those beautiful eyes when he had challenged her earlier he could have sworn she had been as startled to see him as he had been when *she* had first walked in.

Sitting on the low sofa where someone had settled her down with a glass of water, Sanchia glanced up as the door to the private room swung open to admit the tall figure of the barrister who had challenged her.

Alex Sabre. She couldn't remember who it was who had told her his name.

'Hello, Sanchia.' Her throat went dry as she saw that he had closed the door behind him, watched his purposeful, measured stride across the floor. 'I really didn't think you'd still be here,' he said, and then, in a tone that was softly menacing, 'After all, you were quick enough to ditch me last time, weren't you?'

He was standing in front of her now, looking down on her from his commanding height.

'I'm *sorry?*' Sanchia shook her head as though that would somehow clear the fog that seemed to be clouding her senses. In the confines of the quiet room the sheer presence of this man was mind-blowing 'Do—do I know you?' she asked tentatively, frowning. Surely he could only have got her name from being in court?

'Know me?' Some private emotion chased across his hard, handsome face, deepening the groove between those very masculine brows as his eyes scanned her face with the thoroughness of a laser. But then he laughed. A short, sharp sound, devoid of any humour. 'Oh, that's very good! Is the loss of memory permanent? Or was it something you dreamed up when you realised I was the defending advocate? Because, believe me, it was as much a surprise for me in that court just now as it was for you.'

'Surprise?' She couldn't understand what he was talking about.

'Or perhaps that was the intention?' he suggested, cutting across her mind-spinning confusion. 'One final little advantage stroke before you finally agreed to face up to facts.'

'Facts? What facts?' she demanded, still shaking her head.

'You know very well what I mean. Why did you take off the way you did that day? Without a word, without even the courtesy of an explanation! Where did you go? Why were you so determined never to be found?'

'I'm sorry…' she said again, out of confusion rather than apology. She put her hand to her forehead, felt the dull ache that throbbed between her temples.

'I just never dreamt it was so abhorrent to you that you'd actually run away.'

'Run away?' *From what?* Her mind battled in vain for an answer, and through what seemed like a thickening haze came up with nothing except the stirrings of an inexplicable unease. 'Are you sure you haven't made a mistake?' she said shakily.

'A mistake?' He laughed again, even more harshly than before. 'Oh, I made a mistake all right! For goodness' sake, Sanchia! Credit me with some intelligence. How long are you going to keep this up?'

'Keep what up?' she challenged, wondering if it was his daunting anger or something else—something nagging at her memory—that was making her feel vulnerable and afraid. 'The fact that I don't know what you're talking about—don't even know who you are?'

'For pity's sake!' He slapped his forehead with his hand, his head turning sharply so that his profile was exposed to her in all its hard austerity. What did the girl think she was playing at?

Sanchia's head hurt from the effort of trying to remember, her thoughts leaping ahead, making connections, blind assumptions. He was a barrister. She had never mixed with barristers, had she? Why would she have had any dealings with one? Unless...

'Was I a witness, or something? Is that why I ran away?'

'A *witness?*' Something flared in the penetrating grey eyes as he turned back to glare at her with stark incredulity. His teeth were clenched, as though he was doing his level best to hold on to what remained of a frighteningly rigid control. 'No, my dear girl, you weren't a witness. And I don't think I need tell you what I do with those who imagine they can fob me off with lies and generally make an idiot out of me—even with such a first-class performance as you're giving now.'

He would tear them apart.

Though she didn't know him, she knew that much, and she shivered, remembering what she had overheard someone saying about him earlier.

Coming from a family involved in investment and property, he had inherited a fortune on his father's death—which he was well on the way to doubling. Even without the vast professional fees he could command, he didn't need to work. But perhaps he just liked wielding power over people, Sanchia thought distractedly, because apparently he was known in court circles as being triple 'R'-rated. Rich, ruthless and respected. So ruthless that anyone who came up against him who wasn't telling the truth, the whole truth and nothing but the truth, didn't stand a chance.

Now the dangerous softness with which he had spoken sent a violent shudder through her, making her temples pulse with a throbbing pressure. Something stirred in the recesses of her consciousness, a heavy drawn curtain whose dark folds refused to part, no matter how frantically she searched for daylight, for freedom, for clarity.

'I'm not giving any performance!' An eternal frustration brought her own anger welling up inside of her. 'I've already told you! I don't know what you're talking about—or who you are! You say you know me, but I can't remember you! I had an accident and lost my memory. I can't remember you—or anything about you! I can't remember a thing!'

She dropped her head into her hands, groaning as a wave of nausea washed over her. Through the fog of her consciousness she battled to find the truth, the effort making her head feel as though it were splitting in two.

'Sanchia?' He had dropped down on his haunches in front of her. Through the screen of her fingers she could see the pinstriped trousers pulling over his bunched thighs, saw how his robe pooled on the floor behind him like a dark cloak.

'My God...' His tone was strung with disbelief and his face was etched with incredulity as he caught her hands, drawing them down in the determined strength of his. 'If I thought for one moment that you were serious...'

'Of course I'm serious!' she breathed, meeting his eyes on the level. They were cold and glittering and clear. But the intimacy of those hard hands clasping hers caused a sudden quickening of her blood, so that finding herself the focus of such a man made her pull back as though from a tremendous shock. 'Why would I want to lie?'

From the furrow that appeared between his eyes they had registered that disconcerted little action. As they would register everything...

'Do you want to tell me about it?'

Sanchia hesitated. He was a stranger to her, and yet his compelling authority forced her to respond. 'I had an accident. When I was in Northern Ireland.'

'Ireland?' He sounded surprised, but he let her go on.

'I stepped out in front of a car and was knocked unconscious. When I came to I couldn't remember a thing. Not what had happened, where I lived, or who I was. Gradually things began to come back. Things further back in the past. I remember my parents. When they died. Where I was. I remember everything until my late teens. But after that some things remain hazy.' No, not just hazy, she thought. Totally obliterated. 'Sometimes things just don't tie up. Like walking in here today...'

'What about walking in here today?' Restrained urgency overlaid the deep tones.

'Sometimes I feel as though I've done things before, though I know I couldn't have.'

'How do you know you couldn't have done them?'

'I just know,' she answered lamely. 'There's a portion of my life I can't recall, but I can't have done anything that important or significant.'

'How do you know?'

'Because I'm sure I'd remember it if I had. It's just a matter of a year or so. Two, maybe. Like where I was before the accident, what I was doing. I've never been able to find the link.'

'How long were you in Ireland?'

A slender shoulder lifted beneath the fluid jacket of her trouser suit. 'I'm not really sure. I think I'd just moved there before the accident, because I was still in a bed and breakfast.

Apparently I'd told the landlady I was an orphan and totally foot-loose and fancy-free, and that I was using a post office box ad-dress until I got myself some permanent digs.'

'How long have you been back in England?'

'Just a couple of months. I knew I'd lived in London. I just couldn't remember where, or when I'd left, or why. Until then I was afraid to leave the safety of the places I knew. The doctors said things would probably come back in time, given the right stimulus, but…' She gave another dismissive little shrug. 'It's been over two years now, and they haven't. They say there might possibly have been something so traumatic in my life before the accident that my brain refuses to remember it. They call it psy-chogenic amnesia.' Her tone derided the phrase, as well as her own inability to recover from it.

'And you?' He stood up then, with a subtle waft of rather pleasant aftershave lotion. Sanchia was very relieved. Crouched down in front of her like that, his masculinity was far too dis-turbing. 'Do you believe that?'

She shook her head, more out of bewilderment than negation. 'I don't know. I don't know what to think. How can I know?' Vaguely sometimes she thought there must have been some boy; she caught a snatch of a voice, a bleary outline of features, a sus-picion of being cruelly and brutally hurt.

Perhaps she'd gone to pieces afterwards—had a nervous break-down. Who knew what was locked away in the depths of her mind?

'Had you no friends who were able to help you? To try and retrace your steps?'

'Apparently not. The doctors said I'd told the landlady that I'd been travelling round Britain—going where I pleased—but that I was definitely going to settle there in Ireland. They didn't give me any reason to suspect I wasn't telling the truth.' And then as she remembered, 'You said—you'd…been looking for me.' She tilted her face to the strong features that wiped away any trace of the flimsy images in her brain. 'That I ran away. What from? What was I running from?' A cold, sick fear crept through her. She'd always known she'd been running from something.

'...*never dreamt it was so abhorrent to you that you'd actually run away.*'

As the significance of those words hit home, Sanchia lowered her gaze to stare at the floor, as though she would find the answers stamped on the worn polished boards, her thoughts scouring the dark areas of her mind for the worst possible scenario. She had done something awful! Or been accused of it at the very least. 'Were you defending me or something?' The eyes she raised to his were dark with appeal. 'Is that how we know each other? What did I do? Tell me!'

'You didn't *do* anything.' A faint smile touched his mouth and was gone again, like a glimpse of the sun in an overcast sky. 'Nothing unlawful anyway. Though that isn't to say that what you did do, my lovely Sanchia, couldn't be construed as criminal.'

Which meant what? she wondered, swallowing, detecting the inflection in his voice, the biting emotion behind the disturbing way he had addressed her held in check, she sensed, only by a formidable will. Involuntarily her gaze moved over his taut robed body, coming to rest again on the strong, hard contours of his face.

'Who are you?' she asked shakily, suddenly—inexplicably—afraid.

Alex hesitated. To tell her the truth would be to make a mockery of himself if she were just stringing him along with this preposterous story. And if she weren't...

One strong masculine forefinger lifted insolently to trace her cheek, making her breath catch from the disturbing intimacy of his action. 'You really don't remember?'

She shook her head, recognising the disbelief that still laced the deep tones. Her heart was racing in her breast.

'Anything?'

In the stillness of the room his voice, like his touch, was caressingly soft.

She didn't know him, and yet her body responded as though she did—as though he had done this to her before and she had responded in exactly the same way. She closed her eyes at the shocking impulses that rocked her with devastating sensuality.

'Let's just say we…' his hesitation was marked '…were acquainted. Very briefly.'

Her wan features were wary, the only colour a splash of pink along her cheekbones from the mind-shattering awareness that had gripped her just now from the lightest brush of his hand. 'Acquainted?' Mercifully he wasn't touching her any more. 'What do you mean? In what way acquainted?'

He didn't elaborate at once, as though he were weighing her reactions, his every move calculated, geared to eliciting the truth.

She shot him a sidelong glance, nervous again as she asked, 'Were we…dating?'

He gave a short, sharp laugh. *'Dating?'* Was that scorn or simple rejection in his voice?

'I just meant…were we…seeing each other?'

'If that's what you want to call it.'

Oh, good grief! Then did that mean that she…that they…?

'What happened?' she asked tremulously, her throat contracting from the wild imagery her brain had started processing, afraid of the answers without fully understanding why.

'It ran its course.' It wasn't true, of course. Not by a long chalk, Alex thought grimly. But if she really had lost her memory she wasn't ready for the explicit details of their far too brief acquaintance.

He sounded cold and unmoved, Sanchia thought, her mind racing, desperately trying to grasp a thread of memory that faded even before it had taken shape.

Despairingly, she got up, moving over to the window.

In the street below, the city's traffic was flowing unusually freely for a weekday morning in high summer. Pedestrians jostled with each other along the busy street, tourists and workers alike reflect-

ing a world going about its business—while she was marooned up
here, with this man who both terrified and excited her, groping like
a blind person for a safe footing on a slippery precipice.

'How…?' She didn't want to have to ask—couldn't turn
around as she tried to formulate the question that was burning
through her brain, managing eventually to croak, 'Just how…
deeply were we…involved?'

Through the muted sounds in an outer corridor—a man's
sudden cough, the echo of footsteps across the floor—Alex
Sabre's sharp intake of breath was unmistakable. When he spoke,
however, his voice gave nothing away.

'You can't remember?'

She tried. Put her hand to her head. Goodness knew, she
wanted to. Blindly she shook her head.

'If by *involved* you mean were we lovers…?' The unfinished
sentence was laden with meaning.

Sanchia's back stiffened. Violently she shook her head again.
No! Not with him! she thought, every nerve pulsing with an out-
rageously sensual rhythm as her brain determinedly denied it.
She would have known. Remembered something like that.
Remembered him…

'I would have remembered,' she said hopelessly to the window.

In the succeeding silence she was conscious only of his daunting presence, his scent, even his hard, steady breathing, her every
sense painfully acute.

'Sanchia. Turn around.'

She couldn't have done so but for that soft command in his
voice. Even then it was only to fix her troubled, confused gaze
on his white wing collar and tabs, a vivid contrast with the dark
austerity of his gown.

'Don't worry,' he advised, and then, in a tone that was almost
hostile in its coldness, 'I would take your answer from the way
your mind so keenly rejects the possibility.'

She noticed how harshly those masculine features were
etched in the light coming from the window as her shoulders

sagged with almost disproportionate relief. If double-crossed, she thought, he would make a formidable adversary.

'If it puts your mind at rest, I stopped looking for you a long time ago,' he went on. 'Even so, I'd like to help you.'

'Help me?' Amber eyes widened in amazement.

'If, as you say, you've lost a whole chunk of your life, then I'd like to help you try and retrieve it.'

'How?'

'Whatever it takes.'

Others had tried before—doctors, psychiatrists—and with no satisfactory outcome or hope of her memory ever coming back she had discharged herself over six months ago, resigned to the fact that it never would. But was it possible after all this time, she wondered, both fearful and excited by the prospect, that she could regain the lost pieces of her life, as this confident and obviously brilliant man seemed to think?

Whatever it takes, he had said. She shivered, trying not to imagine the methods a man like him might employ to delve into the intricacies of her locked, dysfunctional mind. She was afraid, and yet contrarily, with a bone-deep instinct she couldn't even begin to understand, she knew that in doing so he wouldn't harm her. Not any lasting physical harm, at any rate…

'Why?' Her slanting eyes were guarded as she looked at him askance. 'Why would you want to help me?'

'Why?' The firm lines of the sensual mouth moved as though he were contemplating her question. 'What about because the subject intrigues me? Because *you* intrigue me, Sanchia?'

'Because I—?' There had been an edge to his voice which made her break off, her features harden with sudden challenging anger. 'You don't believe me! You still don't believe me, do you?'

'I didn't say that.'

'No, but you're thinking it.'

'How do you know what I'm thinking when I'm not even sure myself?'

'And you claim to know me.' She wasn't sure why she felt such bitter disappointment, but she did. 'How can you? How can you know anything about me if you think I'd make something like this up?' She wasn't sure of him. She wasn't sure of anything. But one thing she knew was her own character. That couldn't have changed, no matter how many months or years of her life had gone missing. Could it?

'Believe me, I want very much to make sense of it all. To believe you—'

'But you don't!'

She swung back across the floor, her high heels expressing her agitation. She felt that after this she would be walking out of here to face a greater, more frightening void in her life than she could ever have imagined possible.

The loneliness was suddenly terrifyingly overwhelming. A low moan came from her throat like that of an injured animal, but as she made to push past him his arm shot out, his fingers clamping hard around her wrist.

'For heaven's sake, Sanchia! Virtual strangers we might be, but do you really think I'm letting you walk out of here like this?'

'Like what?' Her pulse was hammering crazily under his broad thumb.

'Like a little lost child—not knowing where she's going, let alone where she's come from.'

'Let me go!' she protested as her struggle to free herself only served to tighten his hold on her. 'I was perfectly all right before I came in here today!'

'I don't think you were. When you looked at me in that court you looked...ridden by some sort of terror that could destroy you if it isn't rooted out. Like you were being hounded by some nightmare you couldn't ever wake up from.'

A chilling sensation shivered along her spine. How could he be so perceptive? How could he know?

Shaken, she tried not to let him see how his words—how he—was affecting her as finally she wrenched free from his clasp. 'What do you think you're doing? Psychoanalysing me now?'

A thick eyebrow arched as he noted the disparagement with which she said it, but slipping a hand into the pocket of his well-cut trousers, all he said in response was, 'I gather you've had your fair share of that.'

She didn't need to answer, wondered if the desolation she felt showed in her eyes.

Unwillingly she noticed how the way he was standing, with his robe pushed back, revealed the hard lines of his body. A body honed to peak fitness with the same punishing stamina with which he must have honed that keen intellect—single-minded determination and ruthless resolve.

'I'm not going to hurt you, Sanchia.'

'I know that.' How? How could she know? she wondered hopelessly, and after a moment asked, 'How do I know you're telling me the truth?

'That I know who you are?'

The neat hair that had once felt like tumbling silk beneath his hands gleamed darkly as she nodded. Alex swallowed to ease the pressure that seemed to be restricting his windpipe.

He wanted to tell her. Prove it to her. Take that hunted look out of her eyes by forcing her to remember, because he was beginning to shake off all doubts that this was any performance. And, curse it though he had just now, maybe—just maybe—her loss of memory might work in his favour. He felt unscrupulous, yet decidedly excited by the prospect as he responded, 'To echo your own words: why would I lie?'

Sanchia frowned. Why would he? He was a barrister. Honourable. Respected.

And ruthless.

That other juror's words sent a little shiver down her spine.

'You're going to have to trust me,' he suggested softly.

'Just like that?'

'Just like that.'

'I can't.' It was like a small hopeless plea in the darkness.

'No.' He moved closer to her, his cool, clear gaze penetrating hers, plumbing the depths of her fear and anxiety with merciless precision. 'No,' he repeated, as though coming to some hard decision. 'I don't believe you could. But all I'm asking is that you allow me to see you again—starting with this evening. I'll take you out to dinner. That way you won't even have to worry about being alone with me.' And that would be for the best all round, he decided wryly, for himself, as well as Sanchia. Because he didn't know how he was managing to stand there without reaching for her, pulling her against him, feeling her softness melting against him as he plundered that sweet, moist mouth…

'I can't,' she said quickly, aware of the hint of sarcasm clothing his last remark. Nor did she particularly regret having to say it. Because, much as she wanted to recapture her missing memories, she was afraid of unlocking doors her mind clearly wanted to keep sealed. Which was as ridiculous, she thought, as fearing any kind of involvement with Alex Sabre. But nevertheless she did. 'Not tonight. I've arranged to meet someone tonight.'

'Then you'll just have to ring him and tell him you can't make it,' he replied, causing her hackles to rise. She hated being bossed about. He was also wrong in his assumption that she was seeing another man, but she held back from telling him that. It was none of his business anyway. Before she could say anything, he tagged on, as though he were speaking to a rather stubborn child, 'Isn't this more important?'

Which, of course, it was, she thought, having already decided to telephone her friend to postpone their cinema trip.

'That's settled, then,' he said, and it seemed it was.

CHAPTER THREE

'Wow! No wonder you decided to call off an evening with me in favour of a night out with him!'

Jilly's enthusasm brought Sanchia over to the window, to see Alex Sabre, in casual jacket and dark trousers, just locking his car. It was a shiny black BMW, long and sleek, a statement of his wealth and position.

'He says he can help me,' Sanchia murmured, reiterating what she had told her friend and neighbour earlier, when she had reluctantly postponed their night out at the cinema. 'But I don't know.'

A blonde and bubbly thirty-year-old divorcee, Jilly Boston knew about Sanchia's amnesia. Sanchia had taken the older woman into her confidence quite soon after moving into the small garden flat, when she'd realised what a kind and helpful neighbour Jilly was—always willing to take her photographic deliveries in for her and feed the fish. Now, though, steeling herself to meet Alex Sabre again, she couldn't explain the doubts and fears that were nagging away at the perimeters of her subconscious.

'He says we knew each other—only briefly, by the sound of it—but he's a link with the part of my life that's missing, and I do want to know what I was doing then. Only…'

'Only what?' Jilly prompted gently.

'I don't know why, but I'm afraid.'

'Just because that psychiatrist said that there must be something so traumatic lurking there behind all that grey matter that you've blanked it out, it doesn't mean there is. Perhaps it's completely the opposite, and things were so mundane at that period of your life that there's nothing really significant to remember.' Jilly grimaced. 'I should know. Most of my life is like that.' The self-deprecating quip made Sanchia smile. 'But if a man like that offered to help *me*, I'd lie down at his feet, plead total incapability, and tell him to take all the time he needed.'

Which was so far from the truth that Sanchia burst out laughing.

The nerves that had been eating away at her insides for the past hour, however, had her stomach muscles tightening up seconds later as the doorbell pealed.

'He's here! I'll make myself scarce,' Jilly announced, grabbing the nail lacquer remover she had popped in to borrow. 'And don't worry.' This with a comforting little smile. 'You've already assured me he's a respected barrister. And from the look of him I'd say you were in extremely good hands.'

'Were you having your flatmate look me over?' Alex enquired dryly five minutes later, putting the car into motion as Sanchia secured her seatbelt.

So he had noticed Jilly's interest, she realised, sinking back against the plush grey leather, guessing that there wasn't much that would escape him.

'Jilly isn't my flatmate,' she responded edgily. 'She's my neighbour.'

'And a good friend?'

'Yes. And she wasn't looking you over,' she supplied, rather less truthfully, wishing Jilly hadn't been so obvious in her appreciation of those dark good looks and the compelling authority of this man sitting beside her. 'She was just a little surprised, that's all. I don't normally go out with men like you.' What a stupid thing to say, she chided herself, feeling gauche.

'Oh?' He flicked the indicator switch to signal his intention to turn right at the end of the road. 'What type do you normally go out with?'

Was she imagining it, or was there a sudden abrasive edge to his voice?

Certainly her type wasn't big and commanding and powerful, and he was all of those things, she decided. In fact, over the past couple of years she hadn't really gone out with any men, except perhaps for a blind date someone else had arranged without telling her, and to which she had only reluctantly agreed because it had been in the safe company of friends.

'Not prominent barristers,' was all she offered.

His eyes made a cursory survey of her simple cream top and tailored trousers, sending a small ripple of awareness right down through her body.

'And how do I differ from all the other men you've known?'

Was he kidding?

'You move in different circles, for a start.'

'How do you know what circles I move in?'

Sanchia pursed her lips. She didn't, did she? 'You're also very, very clever.'

'And does that unnerve you?'

Was it that apparent? she wondered despairingly, but said, 'No,' rather firmly, just in case it was. 'It just warns me to be careful, that's all.'

He smiled lazily, a smile that displayed the sheer power of his steel-edged magnetism. 'Why? Because I might uncover things about you that you might not want revealed?'

A little shudder played across her nerves. 'That's your job,' she reminded him, glancing out of the window.

'Only in court,' he said, and then, with a sudden softening in his tone, 'And even then I can be gentle when I need to be.'

But at other times he would be merciless. She didn't need memory to assure her of that.

Nevertheless, a leap of the reckless excitement she had experienced that morning sent her blood accelerating through her veins as her mind processed the scenarios to which his gentleness might extend.

'Do you know of anything in my past,' she asked, suddenly dry-mouthed, 'that I would rather wasn't revealed?'

'Like you robbed banks for a pastime? Or were caught up in some exotic web of intrigue, with any number of double agents after you?'

'I'm serious.'

Straightening the car after taking the junction, he sent her a glance that was hard and searching. 'You tell me.'

Frustration gnawed at her with the cold probability that he might still not wholly believe she was telling him the truth.

'I can't,' she said dully, with a sudden weary slump to her shoulders.

The look he directed at her now was reflective—questioning. 'Then let's just take it one step at a time,' he advised, his voice quiet but firm.

The restaurant to which he took her was an intimate little bistro, patronised Sanchia decided, seeing its popularity, by a regular clientele.

She felt Alex's searching regard as a waiter pulled out her chair for her, supplied them with menus and placed a napkin ceremoniously over her lap.

It was just the place to bring someone on a first date. Relaxed, but with impeccable service, Sanchia thought. Only it wasn't a first date, was it? Or a date of any kind, if it came to that.

She met grey eyes across the table that were watchful, darkly assessing. 'Have I been here before?'

'What do you think?' he said.

Her gaze strayed across the softly lit tables, touched on the decorative climbing plants, the low painted ceiling, the bright, sparkling glasses at the bar. 'I don't know,' she murmured, frowning. 'It seems familiar, but it could just be reminding me of half a dozen other places I've visited. And yet...'

'And yet what?'

'You said you wanted to help me remember, and I don't think you're a man to waste time with anything that doesn't further your immediate objectives.'

An eyebrow lifted in subtle acknowledgement, the smile playing around his mouth not quite reaching those clear, penetrating eyes.

'An accurate assessment of my character, but it does rather make me sound as though I care for very little but my own ends.'

She surveyed him obliquely, her eyes both wary and challenging. 'And do you?'

'Why? Is there something in your subconscious that's warning you to be on your guard against me?'

Was there?

'I don't know,' Sanchia answered truthfully. 'Should there be?'

He laughed. 'This conversation's going nowhere,' he remarked. 'But, yes, I think you'll find you *have* been here before.'

With you? For some reason she bit back the unsettling words. Forehead puckering, she glanced around her again, seeing things that had supposedly touched her life and yet which now bore no testimony to that other time, feeling ghost-like, because nothing intruded on the void, leaving her feeling empty and invisible.

'Sanchia?' From across the table Alex's voice shook her out of the haze that had been threatening to engulf her. Her wrist, lying casually on the table, was encircled by fingers that were warm and strong.

'I don't remember,' she murmured, her bloodless features ravaged from the effort of trying to.

'Are you receiving any treatment that might help you?'

'No,' she admitted, disentangling herself from that disturbing hand.

'Why not?'

So she had to tell him she had given it up as pointless, and saw his eyebrows arch in undisguised criticism. 'Wasn't that a rather foolish thing to do?'

'Perhaps, but *you* try it,' she retorted, acquainting him with the endless sessions of therapy, the eternally false hope and, at the end of it all, the acceptance of defeat, that that part of her life was lost, never to be retrieved. 'I had to get on with my life,' she finished quietly.

'And you think you're doing that?'

'Yes.'

'And making a good job of it?'

'Yes,' she said adamantly.

'You don't ever wonder if you might be missing something of vital importance to you?'

She shrugged. 'I did at first. In fact, for a long time. But I know I don't have any living relatives, so I knew there wouldn't be anyone looking for me or missing me. I don't know why I lost my memory—or even what I was doing before I stepped out in front of that car. Maybe I was stressed out over something— money, my job, a boyfriend—and that's what made me step off the pavement without looking. Or maybe I was perfectly happy and just taking a quiet stroll—I just don't know. But in the end I thought that if the psychiatrist was right, and I *had* been through something so awful that my mind had blocked it out, then perhaps it would be better not to know.'

'Isn't that rather a short-sighted view?'

'A coward's way out, you mean?'

He didn't say as much, although from the compression of his lips he was certainly thinking it.

'Perhaps from where you're sitting that's what it looks like. But I'm perfectly happy as I am, and if my memory doesn't want to come back, why try and make it?'

'And yet you came out with me.'

Across the table their eyes clashed, and something about the dark intensity in his made her pulse throb with the acknowledgement of a powerful sexual chemistry she had recognised from her first glance at him in the courtroom that morning. Although even before she had looked at him she had felt *something*…

However casual their relationship might have been, however

insignificant, she was sure of one thing. That dark fascination he possessed, which must have attracted her to him originally, hadn't died with her lost memories or with time. It flared into vibrant life every time he looked at her, molten and incandescent—and she knew it would consume her with its dangerous power if she let it. She didn't know how she knew that. She just did.

'Yes,' she breathed, answering him now.

'Why?'

Why?

She wanted to tell him lightly that it was out of curiosity that she had accepted his offer of dinner tonight, that it was nice to be invited out, and if he could give her memory a prod in the right direction all well and good. But the pull of his dark attraction rendered her incapable of such a performance, so it was all she could do to suggest rather unsteadily, 'Why don't we talk about you?'

From the smile curving that strong mouth he had obviously guessed why she had changed the subject, but he went along with her, saying, 'All right. What do you want to know?'

'Interests?'

He sat back on his chair, mouth firming before he answered, 'Good literature. Good wine. Good music.'

She laughed. 'Naturally. And you aren't wearing a ring, so I would hope you aren't married.'

His eyes narrowed beneath the thick fringes of his lashes. 'You think that my being here with you might mean I'm cheating on someone else?'

'It isn't unheard of.'

'Rest assured,' he said, sitting forward again, 'I'm not.'

'Any family?' She sipped the aperitif he had bought her from the bar.

'My parents are dead. I still have a stepmother somewhere.'

Somewhere. Was she imagining that sudden hardening in his voice? 'What about brothers or sisters?'

'What about them?'

'Do you have any?' She suddenly felt as though she were wading through mud.

'I had a brother. Half-brother,' he amended, almost distractedly, and reached for his glass.

'Had?' Sanchia prompted cagily, setting hers aside, not sure she should be asking when she saw the lines that were etched into that strong face.

'He believed in living life on the edge. One day it just caught up with him.'

He was watching her, she thought, with eyes that were hurting, yet direct and unfaltering too. 'What happened?' It came out on a whisper.

He glanced down at his glass. 'He took up a plane he wasn't authorised to fly—with disastrous consequences.' As he had done everything he shouldn't have, Alex thought, feeling bitter and torn inside.

'I'm sorry,' Sanchia murmured, sympathising, especially in view of how young he must have been.

A smoothly clad shoulder moved almost imperceptibly. 'Let's talk about something else.'

Obviously Alex was still affected by it, and Sanchia was happy to comply. She was glad that the waiter reappeared just then to take their order, and the next few minutes were spent discussing the various choices on offer.

'That's my favourite,' she remarked, after the waiter had gone, approving the expensive bottle of Sancerre Alex had chosen to accompany their meal.

'Yes,' he affirmed softly, taking her by surprise, until she remembered.

Of course. He knew her—probably knew things about her she hadn't retained any knowledge of herself. Suddenly she felt much too vulnerable, totally and uncomfortably disadvantaged.

Under the soft lighting his hair was gleaming like jet, and the unfastened neck of the black and grey striped shirt he wore beneath his jacket exposed the crisper hair of his body, curling against skin that would tan easily.

Unconsciously Sanchia's gaze slid down over his torso, visualising, as clearly as though she knew every contoured muscle, the lean, hard power and sinewy strength of him beneath those expensively tailored clothes.

Her head swam in a fog while the throb of a base guitar from concealed speakers echoed her heartbeat, providing the sensually hypnotic backing to a sultry ballad.

She was looking at him, Alex thought, like a sleepwalker. She started suddenly, and embarrassed colour crept into her cheeks—as though she had been jolted awake to find him watching her.

'How did we meet?'

Reaching for one of the rolls from the basket the waiter had left at their table, Alex broke it apart and began buttering it, snatching a few moments to try and work out what to tell her, giving himself time. 'You've no glimmer of recollection?'

Sanchia made a hopeless little gesture, saw the lines scoring that strong intellectual forehead.

'It was at a party.'

'A party?'

'Around two years ago.'

'Two years…?' She was starting to sound like an echo, but she couldn't help it. 'I don't remember,' she said despairingly, with her elbows resting on the table, her splayed fingers pressed to her temples as she searched for memories that wouldn't come.

'For me it was a mix of business and pleasure, and you—you were there taking photographs.'

'Photographs? So I was working?'

'No, not that night.'

Sanchia frowned. 'So where was it? Whose party was it?' Her expression was pained with the effort of trying to remember.

'Those details aren't really important for the time being.'

'Was I on my own?'

There was a moment of hesitancy before he answered. 'Yes.'

'I was?' She shook her head, as though the movement could shift the eternal fog that clouded her mind. What confidence she must have had, she thought, because she certainly wouldn't do that now. 'So we met at this party,' she went on contemplatively, 'and…you asked me out?'

Alex's breath felt like a ton weight in his lungs. How could he tell her that he had used her to sate pure animal lust, to relieve himself of the guilt and grief he had been burdened with on the death of his half-brother? He didn't even want to bring up Luke's name.

'Not…exactly,' he answered her, with a kind of grimace.

'Oh?' Sanchia's eyes widened as a startling possibility dawned. 'I asked *you* out?' She couldn't believe she would have had the courage to be that forward with a man like him—knew she wouldn't have in a million years—and she was certain her character couldn't have changed that much. Yet deep down in the recesses of her mind something nagged, worried, rubbed away at the fringes of her consciousness like a scouring pad over a raw wound.

'The night of that party,' Alex was telling her. 'I didn't even find out your name.'

'How come?'

His mouth twitched mirthlessly. 'You didn't seem too disposed to tell me,' he said, his lashes coming down over the steel-grey of his eyes.

'Why not?' She gave an incredulous little laugh. 'Was I playing it that cool?' His revelation amazed her. She couldn't believe she would have acted that way with anyone—least of all a man like him.

He wasn't laughing with her. He was simply watching her. Watching, waiting and assessing her reactions. As he would watch and wait and assess the reactions of those unfortunate enough to come under his hard interrogation in court.

'You probably terrified me,' she admitted with a little shiver.

'Do you find me that threatening, Sanchia?' he asked softly.

She didn't answer. What could she say? *I don't know you. How do I know what kind of man you are?* And yet somehow she felt she *did* know—could tell simply from being with him that behind that air of authority and that mind-blowing sexual charisma was a code of honour he would do his utmost to preserve.

'So what happened after that?'

After that? He didn't know how to handle this. He would always assess the currents, always chart his course, before instigating any line of action. Yet now, for almost the first time in his life, he felt dangerously close to being out of his depth.

He had already misled her about their first meeting—by omission if not with wilful untruths. And yet to tell her the truth at this stage, he thought, curbing a raging frustration to do so, would probably only succeed in driving her from him again. Because what was the truth? That they had nothing on which to build a relationship other than a hopeless abandoned hunger for each other?

'When we met again…it was…under far…different circumstances. I…'

He spoke with some hesitancy, as though he were having difficulty recalling the exact details. As though he'd simply filed the information away as too insignificant to retain, she thought, seeing the dark intensity in his eyes and the lines scoring his forehead as he flipped a mental chart of what must be dozens of discarded girlfriends until he brought up the page marked Sanchia Stevens.

'You were working for a small provincial newspaper. As a freelance photographer.'

'Did I work for a newspaper…?' She shook her head, trying to stir some recollection of that time, but nothing would come.

'I walked into their offices on a day when you happened to be there.'

'Really?' The coincidence made her brows shoot up before she asked, with a nervous little smile, 'And was I more co-operative this time?'

He sat forward, resting his arms on the table. 'You were never co-operative,' he murmured, and there was such dark sensuality in the firm curve of his mouth that a little frisson ran through her.

What had he meant by that?

She didn't doubt that a full red-blooded male like him would be a dynamic and demanding lover. So had he wanted her while she had denied him? Was that what had eventually broken them up?

'So I gave you the run-around for a while,' she decided aloud, and before she could stop herself added, 'But we obviously didn't embark on a long and glorious affair?'

She couldn't believe she had said it—couldn't believe that she was responsible for the predatory smile that tugged at his lips as he returned softly, 'Are you intimating that you wish we had, Sanchia?'

'I didn't say that!' Shaming colour crept up her throat into her cheeks and she knew he would see it and recognise it for what it was. Pure, unadulterated embarrassment. Because surely he couldn't know what she was thinking: that she couldn't possibly have been involved with a man like him without finding herself in the midst of a wildly torrid affair. He was certainly affair material, and had he wanted more than a platonic relationship with her she couldn't imagine how she could have resisted...

'What were you doing at the newspaper office?' she enquired rather breathlessly, for something to say—because what did it matter? All she wanted was to steer the conversation away from the disturbing turn it had taken.

'Oh...' He pursed his lips, his eyes reflective yet watchful. 'Chasing information.'

'For a case?'

'You could say that.'

She nodded, her curiosity not entirely appeased. Everything he said was frank enough, and yet she sensed an evasiveness about him, had the feeling that he was holding something back. Which, of course, he would be if he were trying to help her to remember, she reminded herself. He was opening just the right subjects, applying just the right amount of pressure, without giving too much away—as he knew how to, with all the merciless skill of his profession.

She shuddered violently, wondering how much confidence she must have had to imagine she could play around with a man like him and not come out unscathed. That was if she *had* been involved with him at all. Because how did she know that he was even telling her the truth? That she wasn't simply accepting all he told her because she needed so desperately to believe him? How did she know he wasn't just taking advantage of her vulnerability for some cold and calculated purpose of his own?

'How do I know that what you're saying is true?' she challenged him out loud. She was moving blindly through a maze of obscurity with only this man—this stranger who assured her he wasn't a stranger—as her guide. 'How do I know you knew me? Do you have any photographs of the two of us together?'

He gave the barest of shrugs, his mouth pulling down at the corners. 'Not that I can lay my hands on right at this moment.'

Which was probably a polite way of telling her that he had done what any man would do with photos of an old girlfriend he hadn't been particularly serious about, Sanchia realised. Thrown them away.

She was surprised, therefore, when, pulling something from the inside pocket of his jacket, he passed it across to her, saying, 'I do, however, have this.'

An incredulous little sound left her as she gazed down on a glossy, colourful photograph of herself. She was standing against the stone wall of a building, looking directly at the camera, her hair swept casually up, the warmth in her eyes and the curve of her lips only for the person who had captured her at that moment.

'Did you take this?' she breathed, stunned that he should have it in his possession when she couldn't even remember it being taken.

'I think it proves I knew you,' he stated, without answering her. 'Oh, and there was this.'

A barely audible sound left her as she took the second photograph he handed her. It was a picture of a swan, stretching its wings for take-off. It had been superimposed over another swan that was sculpted out of ice. Against a black background, the real cob appeared to be breaking out of the breast of its frozen twin, so that water splashed up from its powerful wings, representing splintered ice.

'It's beautiful,' she whispered. 'Where did you get it?'

'It was with your photograph.'

An insidious tension stole through her. 'Who took it?'

'What do you think, Sanchia?' he asked quietly.

Across the table their eyes clashed, and something about the dark intensity of his made her heart race, her pulses throb from a glimpse of fleeting memory, something too elusive to capture. It dragged a desperate little sound of defeat from her.

The music around them had changed to a pulsing, exotic beat, and something inside her head felt as though it were about to snap.

She covered her face with her hands, breathing deeply to control the fear and panic that were suddenly sweeping over her.

'What's wrong?' The concerned tones came from what seemed like a great distance away. Distractedly she sensed him retrieving the photographs she had dropped on the table.

'I don't know. I...' Dizzily she struggled against threatening nausea, breaking into a cold, clammy sweat.

'What is it?' he prompted again.

'I'm sorry.' She glanced up at him over her cupped hands, her eyes huge, their glittering depths the only colour in her otherwise blanched face. 'I'm so sorry... Could we get out of here?'

'Of course.'

Weak-limbed, she struggled to her feet, wondering how she would have stayed on them if Alex hadn't suddenly been there with an arm across her back. Grateful for the support of his strong body, she let him escort her outside.

In the car park she slipped out of his disturbing hold to lean against the wall of the restaurant, breathing deeply, thankful for the cool, revitalising air.

A group of people arriving were looking at her curiously, but she felt too shaken to worry about what they thought.

'What was it?' Alex pressed.

'I don't know.' Her head was swimming. She didn't want to have to think. To be forced into opening her mind to things she knew could hurt her.

'Yes, you do.' His voice was quietly relentless. 'It was something to do with that photograph, wasn't it?'

'No!'

'What was it?' She felt the pressure of his fingers bite into the tender flesh of her upper arm. 'What did you remember?'

'I didn't!' Her features were contorted with the dread that was engulfing her. 'It wasn't anything. Only a feeling. Oh, Alex, please! Don't make me! I can't do this! I just can't go there!'

His grip relaxed, his fingers gentling as they moved along her arm. 'What are you afraid of?' he enquired hoarsely.

'I'm not afraid,' she lied, straightening against the cool, uneven stone of the building in an effort to steady herself, try and regain her composure. But that masculine hand was moving around her waist, and she gave a small gasp when he pulled her gently but determinedly against him.

'You probably think I'm a bully and a heel, and that I should very probably be minding my own business,' he said, 'but trust me.' The rich timbre of his voice was like a caress across her senses. 'I won't make you do anything you don't want to do.'

But he was, she thought hectically. The sensations caused by his hard warmth were creating havoc with her reasoning and her judgement, making her head swim in a maelstrom of dangerous longing.

Twelve hours ago she hadn't known he existed, yet her arms were lifting with a will of their own to cling to his hard strength. Her face was turning now—as though it were second nature—into the soft, warm cushion of his shoulder.

She couldn't contain a small murmur of satisfaction. Dear heaven, he was so good to lean on! She wondered what it would be like to lean on him not just physically, but emotionally too—as those desperate souls who paid a fortune for the benefit of his brilliant mind would lean on him—found herself aching for the support of his mental strength, his confidence, his dependability, aching for the comfort of his physical energies as he...

With sudden shocking clarity she realised the path down which her thoughts had led her, knew without even knowing how that it was an ill-advised path, studded with cautionary signposts every step of the way. But the graze of his jaw against hers and the clean spicy scent of him seemed to have intoxicated her to the point where she couldn't think straight, so that by the time she realised how far she had come she couldn't have retraced her steps even if she had wanted to.

CHAPTER FOUR

AND THEN she was welcoming the mouth that came down hard over hers, responding to the savage hunger of his kiss in almost desperate, mindless abandonment.

She had wanted this! From the moment he had faced her in the court that morning, she knew that, crazily, she had wanted nothing else but this man's arms around her. Now the reality seemed to produce an explosion somewhere deep down inside her, igniting her quiescent body into flaming life.

It was a mutual meeting of mouths, unrestrained and demanding in its intensity.

Greedily, Sanchia's fingers clawed at the rough texture of his face, finding their way into his thick dark hair to weld her mouth to his, her body submitting to his warm hard strength as if it had been made for it.

She heard herself groan, moving her head to do what she had been wanting to do all day and taste the heated skin of his throat. She felt him shudder from the sensations she could feel ripping through him, her body twisting beneath the skill of his hands, welcoming the intimacy they were creating that thrilled even as it shocked her—because she knew she had invited this, had done nothing to even try to stop it.

'No!' Forcibly she managed to pull herself free. 'I'm sorry. I didn't mean to do that. I got carried away. I—' She was blabbering and she knew it, feeling the cold absence of his arms suddenly almost as profoundly as her stinging shame. 'I shouldn't have let you do it.'

Flushed, his chest rising and falling heavily, Alex was staring at her incredulously, though his features seemed set almost in stone.

'Could you have stopped me?' It must be the release of aggressive male desire, Sanchia decided, that caused that tremor in his voice—a voice that was roughened by passion. 'Could either of us have prevented it?'

'I—I don't understand.' She was breathless, bewildered, confused. She only knew that since their very first meeting this morning she had felt an attraction to him more devastating than anything she could ever have imagined. 'Just what sort of relationship did we have before?'

Breathing hard as he was, it seemed to take an age before he answered. But then, as he recovered himself, his lashes came down over the febrile glitter in his eyes, and in a voice that was remarkably controlled after what had just happened, he said, 'We scarcely knew each other.'

And she had responded to him as though he were a long-lost lover! Briefly her eyes closed against her confused embarrassment.

'Don't feel too bad about it,' she heard Alex say, and it jolted her eyes open with disturbing *déjà vu*—as though there had been some similar exchange of words between them before. A sort of cold cynicism had crept into the deep tones. 'We were both equally responsible.'

But that was just it, Sanchia thought, too ashamed to raise her eyes beyond his expensive casual shoes. She *hadn't* been responsible. She had been way, way out of control, and could only explain her response to him with the way she had been feeling at that moment. The way she always felt when the past threatened to surface and submerge her—lost, vulnerable and alone, while he seemed so strong, so self-sufficient, so dependable. And, being a prime male animal, he'd naturally take what was being offered.

Despondently she lifted her head, 'Would you take me home?' It was all she wanted to do, could think of to say.

'I'm sorry about your meal,' she said, when Alex was pulling up outside the flat, and managed a rather wan smile. 'You'll start to wish you'd never agreed to help me.'

'Let me be the judge of that.' Pulling the handbrake on, he turned towards her, his arm coming to rest on the back of her seat. 'And I took you out tonight because I wanted to do just that. Not to indulge any special culinary appetites. But one thing today has shown me is that you're not fit enough to carry out two weeks of compulsory jury service. I've already arranged an exemption for you.'

'You've done what?' Sanchia stared at him, flabbergasted. 'On whose authority?' Trying to help her reclaim her memory was one thing, but she didn't like how he seemed suddenly to be taking control of her life.

'It affected you badly today,' he stated matter-of-factly, 'and you know it did. You'll need a medical certificate to back it up, but you won't have to attend as originally summoned.'

'I'm not an invalid!' she protested, too conscious of that strong arm resting so uncomfortably close, of his daunting presence in such a confined space, the way the shadows that had fallen since they had left the restaurant made him look like the dark satanic lover of some Gothic play. 'I think I can make my own mind up about what's bad for me or not.'

'And you think treading on territory you know nothing about is wise?'

'What do I need to know?' she argued, knowing he was right, yet feeling the need to safeguard her own actions, her independence. 'All I had to do was sit there and—'

'But you couldn't do it.'

No. He'd recognised that much, she thought, wondering if anyone had actually told him she had fainted. Such sharp perspicacity sent a little dart of fear arrowing through her.

'Had I been there before?' she queried, pondering over it. 'Been involved in a case, do you think?'

He laughed then, very softly and said, 'I hardly think so. 'The problem's probably associative. But if you want me to help you, then you'll do as I say.'

There he was again, coming over all authoritative—as though he was an expert on the subject, as though he had every right.

'I wasn't the one who asked for your help,' she reminded him pointedly, feeling uncomfortably manoeuvred.

'No, but you need it,' he answered, killing her argument stone-dead. As he would in court, she imagined, with an intractable witness, slicing through any opposition with the skill of a master.

She wanted to rebel against such high-handedness. But what was the point? she thought, biting her tongue. He was right, wasn't he? She needed all the help she could get.

'Now, if you're really sensible, after a day like you've had today you'll go in there...' his chin lifted towards the house '...and get an early night. And I wouldn't make any dates for a while.'

Which meant what? That he intended taking her out himself? she wondered, with her heart-rate increasing. She was about to challenge him, deciding that on this point at least he had gone too far. After all, who she went out with was no concern of his. Even if there wasn't anyone serious in her life at the moment, and nor did it seem likely there would be in the foreseeable future.

He was already getting out of the car, though, which obviated any chance of an immediate protest. And as he left her at her door, without even attempting to kiss her again, she watched his car disappear, with a brooding look in her eyes and the chilling premonition that with Alex Sabre her problems might only just be beginning.

Alex cursed himself all the way back to his apartment. He had been a fool to take Sanchia to that restaurant tonight, and he wasn't sure whether it had been solely to try and help her or to satisfy his own naturally suspicious mind. He had to admit that he still hadn't been sure whether she had just been playing some foolish little game with him. He had merely been tagging along with her, thinking that she'd give up what he had suspected was a ridiculous charade eventually. But his doubts about whether she was telling the truth had certainly been dispelled by her reaction to that photograph. There was no doubt in his mind now that her amnesia was frighteningly real.

His grip tightened on the wheel as he brought the big car through the familiar luxurious suburb, his body aching with hard, unadulterated need.

He had wanted her tonight—wanted her more than he had ever done—and his loins still ached from the desire that had racked him in that car park. She had wanted him too. She hadn't known why, or even welcomed that crazy cataclysmic response—which was no more than he could expect, he reminded himself with bitter truth. In fact he probably stood a better chance with her if she *didn't* remember.

Nevertheless, it didn't stop him wondering whether he should have been more open with her. There were things she needed to know—things it was important she remembered.

Suddenly the urge to call her—or turn the car around and drive back and force her to accept the things her mind was blotting out—was almost too much to resist. But with a hard steeling of his indomitable will, he forced himself back in control.

How could he know what any sort of outright disclosure might do to her? The mind was a very complex thing, and he didn't want to run the risk of doing anything that might cause her permanent harm, or drive her further into that haven of obscurity to which she had subconsciously retreated. Nor did he want to say anything that would send her running. Just one false step, one careless remark on his part, he suspected fearfully, and she'd be gone—lost to him again—and there was no way that he intended to let that happen.

Because how could he tell her that he had meant nothing in

her life? That, driven by his own demons, he had used her when she had been at her most vulnerable? That he'd never flattered himself he'd been anything but a substitute for someone else? She wouldn't welcome hearing any of that. Any more than she would welcome hearing the other information he had decided for the time being to withhold. That when he had found her in that little newspaper office that day, not by chance, but after weeks of exhaustive searching, he had found her guarded and resisting—and nearly four months pregnant with his child.

Sanchia awoke with a thumping headache, a sore throat, and aching all over.

Which was her body's way of getting her to comply with Alex Sabre's suggestions—or rather orders, she thought grimly. Even if she did have half a mind to defy them and take herself off to court as she had wanted to do.

She was still in her blue silk pyjamas when Jilly called in on her way to work to return her bottle of nail lacquer remover.

'I thought I heard you moving about. You look ghastly!' her friend exclaimed, following as Sanchia padded barefoot back into the living room. 'So much for a night out with a tall, dark, handsome stranger! Did you find out any more about him? Or, more to the point, about yourself?'

'Only that I met him at a party, that I used to work for a newspaper, and that I have an aversion to swans,' she murmured absently, still wondering what it was about that photograph that had set off those panic buttons inside her head. *And that I'm so attracted to him I couldn't get to sleep last night for thinking about that kiss!*

'Swans?' Jilly dropped the little plastic bottle into Sanchia's hand as her friend turned round. 'Were you bitten by one or something?'

'Or something,' Sanchia murmured with a grimace.

'You're talking in riddles,' Jilly castigated her affectionately, picking up a particularly fine enlargement of a nuthatch clinging to a tree trunk. Birds were Sanchia's speciality.

'Am I?' Sanchia put her hand to her throat. It felt as if she had swallowed a whole pack of razorblades. 'That's how I feel. A total conundrum it will take patience and ingenuity to solve.'

'Things I would imagine this Alex Sabre probably has by the ton.'

Sanchia pulled another face. 'Add forcefulness, arrogance and calculating intelligence to that, and you've probably got him in one.'

Returning the photograph to Sanchia's table, Jilly glanced up, interested. 'Do I detect a hint of rebellion in your tone?'

'Not just a hint,' Sanchia assured her, folding her arms as though to strengthen her point.

'Wow! It's about time some man managed to stir you out of that apathy you've had towards the opposite sex for goodness knows how long! Certainly for the whole of the time *I've* known you.'

'Not funny, Jilly.' Moving over to the table, Sanchia straightened a pile of mounts she was in the process of sorting through. 'You know I'm far too busy. I don't know what happened in my life, but I do know that it cost me dear in some ways—financially being one of them. If ever I was financially sound—which I doubt.'

'Didn't he tell you anything else? Like you'd gone to prison for shooting your ninety-two-year-old millionaire lover or something?'

Sanchia couldn't help but smile. 'I seriously don't think he knows that much,' she admitted. And then, because something had been worrying her ever since she had left that restaurant last night, she took a deep breath and said, 'Jilly. You know about men, don't you?'

'Know about them?' Jilly gave one of her cynical laughs. 'What I don't know you could write on a postage stamp.'

'What would make me afraid of as well as attracted to a man I don't even know?'

'Ah-ha!' Jilly exclaimed, repositioning the strap of her shoulder bag over her dark tailored jacket. 'So you're admitting you *are* attracted to him?'

'Don't be *silly*,' Sanchia responded, her tone and her grimace conveying that, realistically, any woman who wasn't attracted to Alex Sabre had to be blind—or dead.

'You mean besides those astounding good looks, that awesome personality and that voice that could melt chocolate?' Jilly's nose wrinkled as she shook her head. 'I've really no idea. Unless it's the forcefulness of his character that you think might suck you into something you don't want to be sucked into.'

'I'm serious, Jilly.' Sanchia dropped down onto the arm of her settee. 'The strength of it frightens me.'

'It's only natural. He's sexy. He's rich. He's powerful. That's a lethal combination And he's offered to help you. No woman could be blamed for falling under the spell of all that. Emancipated and independent we might be, but the need for a protector is strong—if not for ourselves, then for our young. And in your case it must be stronger than in most.'

A sound just outside made them both turn towards the hall.

'I was going straight out. I left the front door open,' Jilly whispered, her jaw dropping and her eyes apologetic as the compelling figure of Alex Sabre loomed in the doorway of the flat.

'Very considerate, Jilly.'

His use of her name caused a questioning glance to pass between both women as Sanchia jumped up, her face expressing only one horrified thought. *How long had he been standing there?*

His smile for Jilly blazed pure charm. 'I wouldn't want to keep you,' he said, his tone pleasant but dismissive.

Jilly grimaced knowingly at Sanchia before lifting unusually flushed features to the dynamic strength of those eyes now surveying her as though she were suddenly superfluous to requirements.

'In that case I'll step down, m'lud.'

She breezed out, leaving Sanchia flinching when the movement of a dark-suited arm closed the door after her.

Dressed for action in that pristine suit, impeccable white shirt and tie, he looked much too commanding—too worldly and handsome—for her modest little flat. Instinctively, she took a couple of steps back.

'What are you doing here?'

One perceptive glance took in the room, with its photograph-adorned walls, the second-hand settee with its untidy cushions, her little tank of tropical fish.

'That isn't much of a welcome after I've fought my way across town specifically to see you.'

'Checking up on me?' she croaked, ragingly self-conscious about this immaculately dressed man seeing her still in her py-jamas, looking so dreadful.

'Do I need to?' he queried smoothly, his sensual appraisal of her beneath the blue silk causing her to break out into a sweat.

She shook her head and winced, reminded painfully of her headache.

'What's wrong?' he asked, quick to notice, a couple of strides bringing him disconcertingly close.

'You got your way. I'm not fit for duty,' she returned in a rasp-ing voice, wondering why it should matter so much that he should see her looking and sounding like this when there he was—the epitome of excellence in every possible way. 'So you can go about your business, getting those desperate souls off the hook like the Demon Defender I've heard you are.' It was how someone else in the jurors' waiting room had referred to him the previous morning.

He didn't make any comment, as he hadn't when Jilly had made that rather inane remark earlier, instead merely lifting a hand to her burning forehead. The action seemed to trap the breath in her very lungs. 'You have a temperature,' he observed.

His palm felt cool against her fevered skin, and she detected faint traces of the aftershave lotion he used still lingering on his fingers. 'Yes.' She had to close her eyes against it, seized by an all too vital picture of him slapping the lotion onto his face, of the way his long fingers would shape that freshly shaven jaw in a way that was wholly masculine; totally erotic.

No!

Sanchia's eyes shot open.

'What is it?' he asked quietly, letting his hand fall.

'Nothing.' Her loose hair moved like silk as she shook her aching head several times, wondering why he always made her feel like this. So tense. So unsettled. So...out of control.

Outside in the street, she heard Jilly's car give a little cough, then start up.

'Have you had a holiday recently?'

The deep male voice broke through the turmoil inside her. 'A holiday?' She frowned, thrown by his question. Finding herself able to breathe again, she stepped away from him. 'No, I haven't,' she responded, wondering if he thought she looked as though she needed one. 'Working for myself, it isn't always easy to. And finances haven't exactly permitted it over the past couple of years.'

'Then it's time you took one.'

'I couldn't agree more!'

'I'm serious,' he said, his tone chastening because he could see that she wasn't. 'The summer recess is coming up, and I'll be going to Bermuda for two or three weeks. I'd like you to come with me.'

'To Bermuda?' Her whispered disbelief hung on the air with the diminishing engine noise of Jilly's little car. Wide amber eyes studied him incredulously. 'With you?'

'Is that so strange a request?'

'Yes.'

'Why?'

'Because I—I don't know you,' she admitted, her breathing shallow.

Something flickered for a moment in the ice-cool depths of his eyes. 'Then it'll be a chance for you to get to know me. For us to get to know each other,' he amended, with a smile that somehow didn't quite reach those stunning irises. 'Perhaps a little bit better than we did before.'

Sanchia's fingers closed tightly around the little plastic bottle she was still holding. 'How much better?' she demanded, her heart-rate quickening.

A broad shoulder lifted beneath the immaculate jacket. 'I think we should just leave that to the gods.'

She had a pretty clear suspicion of what that meant!

'And supposing I don't want that? I haven't exactly done anything to make you think—'

'Haven't you?'

Oh, grief!

'From the way you responded to me in that car park last night, I think your body's being more honest with me than your mind is.'

'That's not true!'

'Isn't it?'

'I don't want to talk about it,' she said.

'No,' he accepted, and something in his tone brought her gaze searchingly to his. His expression was shuttered, though the lines of his mouth and jaw were grim. 'Primarily, my main concern is getting your memory back,' he stated tersely.

Was it? 'And is Bermuda all part of the therapy?'

'I have a friend there. A psychiatrist.' He was watching her closely, eyes cold and clear and beautiful. 'I'd like her to take a look at you. But chiefly it's a holiday—already planned—which I fully intend taking,' he stated decisively. 'But if that means leaving you on your own in your current state—*that* I'm not prepared to do. Nor am I intending to cancel. So that leaves only one alternative. And, as Jilly so aptly pointed out just now, you need protecting more than most.'

He had heard that!

'Yes,' he said quietly—firmly—and she wasn't sure whether he was confirming it or just quashing her protest about needing a protector before it could leave her lips. Disconcertingly, she decided it was probably both.

'So you'll come?'

'I didn't say that.'

'Don't think about it,' he said. 'Just do it. Do you have a passport?'

'Yes, I have a passport.'

'Good. We'll talk about it later. In the meantime I'll make the necessary arrangements.'

'Now, just a minute.' It was all moving way too fast for her. It felt as though he was sweeping the ground from under her feet. 'I haven't agreed to anything. And if I had, there'd still be the matter of a tiny little thing like cost! I can't go halfway round the world—'

'Three and a half thousand miles. Hardly halfway round the world,' he remarked.

'It doesn't matter. I couldn't even afford to go halfway round the country!' she snapped, wishing she hadn't had to spell it out. She felt like a pauper. And she wasn't. Not really. But the way he was looking at her in that hard, disbelieving manner didn't help at all.

'You won't have to,' he said. 'All your expenses will be paid.'

'You mean you'll be paying them for me?'

'That's exactly what I mean.'

'Why?' She sent him a glance. 'Why would you do that? Why would you want to take me somewhere so expensive-sounding as Bermuda without expecting any form of repayment?'

'Oh, I didn't say I didn't expect *any* form of repayment.' His hand lifting to cup her chin, he ran a broad thumb idly across her full lower lip, his smile mocking, his touch stimulating her responses, causing her breathing to quicken, her senses to sharpen into aching acuity as he murmured, in thickly seductive tones, 'Be assured. I'll extract payment—eventually.'

CHAPTER FIVE

SHE came in the end. Against her continual doubts and her better judgement, she consented to Alex's wishes and accompanied him to Bermuda.

Whatever he demanded of her in return, Sanchia decided, she would deal with when—and if—the time came. In the meantime, the prospect of two or three weeks on a sub-tropical island in the North Atlantic looked like fun—even if Alex Sabre did ignite feelings in her that she wasn't sure she welcomed. But she was inexplicably drawn to him in more ways than she wanted to admit. And he was, after all, the only link she had with the missing part of her past.

'Well? What do you think?' Sitting beside her in the taxi, Alex indicated the stunning panorama of distinctive white-roofed houses and the bluest ocean washing the sweeping curve of an incredibly pink beach.

'It's amazing!' she breathed, looking, he thought with gratification, like a child—all wide-eyed and full of wonder. But he could understand how she felt. He had seen this island many times before, yet still it touched him as no other place ever had. 'It's all so…colourful!' she added appreciatively.

He laughed. 'Already mapping out the angles and exposures you'll need for that camera of yours?'

'I'm working on it.' She turned to him again now, eyes glitteringly amber. 'And I really am glad you asked me here.' Once during the past two weeks, when she had seen less of him than she'd expected as he'd been handling a particularly difficult case, she recalled him saying that he visited the island often. That he even had clients here. Obviously very wealthy clients, she decided, otherwise they would never have been able to afford him. 'It's all so fresh and new, and yet...'

'And yet what?' He was half turned towards her, studying her intently, his arm lying casually across the back of her seat.

She was looking out of the window, her face suddenly etched with tension, her eyes trained on the pink canopies of some pedalos on the blue water and the bobbing heads of the bathers taking a cooling dip. 'I don't know...'

He caught that edge of unease that had crept into her voice. Dear God, he prayed desperately. Not yet...

His other hand reached out, gently encircling hers. 'I thought we could get settled in, get changed and fit in a swim before dinner. How do you fancy that?'

'A swim?'

She was a child again, her eyes lighting up as though he had just offered her some unexpected treat. His broad shoulders almost sagged with relief. 'Does that appeal?'

'No.' Sanchia laughed, unsettlingly aware of that warm hand covering hers. 'But I think I can manage to put up with it.'

He was laughing in response, looking more relaxed suddenly. She had sensed a restlessness about him since just before their plane had begun its descent to the airport.

'Hold my hand if you're scared,' she had jested, not for one moment imagining that such a strong, dynamic man would be at all concerned about flying. But he had taken her hand anyway, tucking it under his arm in a way that had been demonstrative and possessive, and, leaning close so that he could be heard above the drone of the powerful engines, he had murmured huskily, 'Ever been dropped from thirty-five thousand feet?'

The teasing in his voice had sent that familiar excitement licking along her veins, which had only resulted in his soft laughter when she dragged her hand free, unable to deal with it. Just like now. Only this time he didn't release the hand she tried to draw away, lifting it to his lips instead.

Audibly, Sanchia caught her breath. His action was so tender—so incredibly erotic—that suddenly this beautiful island with its stunning views and its warm breezes rushing through the car's open windows was somehow diminished as discerning grey eyes—slumberous and heavy-lidded—lifted, capturing hers.

Her pulses seemed to clamour above the melody of birdsong along the tree-lined road, beating like the wings of the humming insects on the scented air.

If any looks could ensnare, then his could, Sanchia thought, enthralled by the sheer power of his sexuality. But it was more than just the physical. It was everything about him. His mind. His body. That indefinable aura of power and authority…

She was relieved when the taxi suddenly turned off the road, stopping at the end of a drive hemmed on either side by oleander trees.

The air bathed her with its warmth as she stepped through the door Alex held open for her and gazed up at what was clearly a private residence.

She shot him a puzzled look, holding back as their driver made short work of retrieving their cases from the back of the car and carrying them up the wide steps to the front porch.

'I—I thought we'd be staying in a hotel.'

'Did you, now?' Casually Alex produced his wallet and extracted several notes to pay the driver. 'Why stay in a hotel when I have a perfectly good house here, sitting idle?'

'It's yours?' Sanchia breathed, flabbergasted. *Perfectly good* was an understatement!

The best in modern architecture, with balconies and pale ochre walls draped in bougainvillea, the house gave onto lush tropical gardens, while beyond she glimpsed the smooth golden crescent of a private beach sloping down to a small jetty, where a speedboat was moored against the glittering backdrop of the sea. It was big, breathtaking, and very, very secluded. Much too secluded, Sanchia thought, swallowing.

'Don't worry,' Alex advised, repocketing his wallet as the other man, after thanking him for the generous tip, shut the door of the taxi and drove off. 'I keep a minimal staff who I'm sure will offer you protection from me—if you feel you need it.'

If she felt she needed it! She wasn't sure whether it was protection from him or from her body's reckless responses to him that she needed, she realised hopelessly, picking up on his cynical tone as he gestured for her to precede him up the steps to the richly polished cedar of the front door.

They were met at the top of the steps by a middle-aged Bermudian woman whose sparkling dark eyes and dusky skin, along with her well-preserved figure, testified to her having once been a real beauty.

'Welcome back, sir.' Her formal address had Sanchia sneaking a wry look at him, which he ignored. But then he was probably used to such deference, she decided with a mental grimace. At home as well as abroad. 'Welcome to our island, Miss—?'

'Sanchia,' Sanchia cut in quickly, refusing to stand on ceremony, offering Alex's housekeeper her hand.

'And is this your first time to Bermuda?' she asked Sanchia with genuine interest, her handshake firm and warm, her fingers feeling slightly weathered.

'Yes. That is—' She broke off, floundering. Saying *I think so* wouldn't augur well for her credibility!

'Every time's a first time in Bermuda, Crystal, you know that,' Alex supplied easily, coming to her rescue and the smile to which he treated them both was enough to buckle any woman's knees.

Another maid joined them and a schedule was discussed briefly before Alex, declining any help with the cases, guided Sanchia upstairs.

The house was a bright, airy labyrinth of spacious rooms—some with ocean views, she noticed, glimpsing them through open doors, and all embellished with classic furniture and paintings and the same rich polished cedar as the hall and stairway—obviously a wood indigenous to the island.

'And so to the bedroom…'

Alex put one of the cases down to open a door off the main landing, and Sanchia gulped as he followed her in, setting hers down beside a huge double bed.

'Won't they think it odd that you've got a woman here but that we're sleeping in separate bedrooms?' she enquired huskily as he moved over to the door of the *en suite* bathroom and pushed it open, assessing, checking things inside. He came back into the room, unbuttoning his shirt as he crossed to open the Venetian blind to the soft rays of the early-evening sun. 'We *are* sleeping in separate rooms?' Despite her anxious question, a coil of excitement was snaking its way through her blood, bringing her tongue to her top lip as her gaze locked unintentionally on the crisp dark hair of the very masculine chest he had practically exposed.

'Why?' Looking at her standing there, with her pink tongue moistening her soft lips and those full breasts rising too tantalisingly under the soft casual shirt, Alex hesitated, racked by an aching desire.

Dear Lord, how could he cope with this? He should have realised how utterly foolish this whole idea was when he had decided upon it, should have booked her—booked them both—into a hotel, as she had in good faith been fully expecting him to do. As it would have been wisest to do—if not for her sanity then most certainly for his.

'Were you expecting that we weren't?' Even to his own ears his voice sounded ragged—hoarse. 'Are you suggesting I ask Crystal to change the arrangements?'

'No!'

'I didn't think so.' The hard cynicism in his voice now made

Sanchia flinch, bringing her provocatively bright eyes to his in wounded challenge. 'And I haven't *got* you here, as you so detrimentally put it,' he said, a little more softly. 'I invited you here as my…guest. And because I thought you could use some fun and relaxation while we try and tackle whatever's lurking in that shuttered mind of yours.'

'I'm sorry,' she said, hoping she hadn't sounded too ungrateful. 'It's just that…I thought…'

'You thought what?' he prompted, the directness of his gaze immensely unsettling.

He had unbuttoned his shirt fully now and Sanchia moistened her lips again, her eyes drawn to the line of dark hair that arrowed down to his taut waist and disappeared somewhere beneath his waistband. She swallowed, heard the blind against the open window rattle softly in the warm breeze. 'That you were planning for us to share a bed.'

'Of course I'm planning for us to share a bed!' His retort echoed like a gun-shot in the otherwise silent room. 'If you hadn't noticed, there's a pretty strong chemistry between us, and, deny it as much as you will, it's going to see its demands are met—sooner or later. I can, however, manage to govern my carnal appetites for the time being—especially with a woman on whom I made such a small impression the first time she doesn't even remember me!'

His swift, surprising anger caused Sanchia to wince. 'That's not very kind,' she reproved him softly, hurt more than she was prepared to let him see.

'Kindness isn't one of my greatest virtues, Sanchia,' he said, his features bleak and forbidding. 'It never was.' He sighed heavily, the action taking some of the tension out of the hard lines of his face. 'But I agree. That was uncalled for. Forgive me.'

It was sexual frustration talking. She wasn't so naïve she couldn't realise that. She could see it in the hard, febrile glittering of his incredible eyes, in the taut, sensual lines of his mouth.

Nevertheless, she inclined her head in silent acceptance, her eyes still wary, her body stiff with unease.

'Relax,' he drawled, unquestionably aware. 'I'm not intending to slake my lust on you, if that's what you're worried about.' His mouth lifted at one corner just a little. 'Not for the time being at any rate. So don't worry. I think I can manage to keep my hands off you for as long as is absolutely necessary. In the meantime…' he moved back across the room, swinging her suitcase up onto the bed as he did so '…let's not waste this perfect evening. I'll see you down in the pool in five minutes.'

'*Five?*' She would have liked to cream off her stale make-up before undressing and rummaging around in her suitcase for her swimwear. But he wasn't allowing her time. 'Can't we make that sooner?' she challenged, still disconcerted by his suggestion that winding up in the same bed was a foregone conclusion.

'Five,' he stressed from the doorway. 'We've got a table booked for dinner, so we have to leave in just over an hour.'

A table? So he was taking her out?

'Five minutes it is then…sir,' she couldn't help tossing after his broad back, in her relief at realising that she wouldn't be spending the evening entirely alone with him.

The swim was good. A cool, refreshing stretching of muscles and easing of tensions after the long flight—and the even longer day.

The only difficulty, Sanchia found, was keeping her mind off the magnificent physique of the man with whom she was sharing the tepid blue water. When she'd come out of the house, discarded her mules and crossed the sun-warmed tiles of the patio, he had just completed several punishing laps of the large pool.

'What kept you?' he had queried lazily, tossing his hair out of his eyes and leaning back against the edge to watch her approach with undisguised masculine appreciation.

She wasn't sure whether it was because she'd suddenly felt naked, wearing what amounted to just three skimpy triangles of sky-blue satin, or if it had been the sight of his hard, muscle-toned torso glistening bronze beneath the water that had made her voice quiver as she answered, 'A desire not to be ordered about?'

'Really?' He grinned, but paid for it when she reached for the nearest thing to hand, which was a towel on one of the sunbeds, and tossed it unceremoniously at his head. It hit him square across his face, as she had intended, and she paid for it in turn when he leapt up and caught her wrist, pulling her off-balance, bringing her shrieking and protesting into the pleasantly cool water beside him.

'Now what was that again?' His tone promised something dangerously exciting. 'I also seem to recall some cheeky little remark upstairs.'

Clutching at his arm, she gave another shriek as she read his very real intention to up-end her.

'No, please…!'

He laughed. 'Begging for mercy?' His lopsided smile implied that none was likely to be granted.

'No!'

The water thrummed in her ears and all went blurred as he treated her to a sudden swift ducking.

'Had enough?' he challenged deeply when she surfaced, gasping, drenching him as she tossed her soaked ebony hair out of her eyes.

'No,' she shot back in reckless defiance, with little spears of pleasure ripping through her as she realised she was actually enjoying provoking him like this, that there was foolish excitement in the thought of what she might incite him to do.

'No!' she screamed again, guessing that she was in for another ducking. Except that this time she grabbed at his powerful biceps, gasping as the action brought her soft body into shattering contact with the long hard warmth of his.

She made a small sound in her throat, something between a purr and a sob as his hand came around the tight tapering line of her waist.

Everything inside her was fighting him, and yet she wanted this as much as he did, Alex realised, powerfully aroused as his hand slid up over the silken flesh of her ribcage. He felt the soft outer swell of her breast under his thumb, saw her head tip back, her eyes close with the desire that held her rigid, and yet he saw painful denial too, before he bent his head to the dangerously erotic perfume of her throat.

Sanchia sucked in her breath. The spell he was weaving around her was as tangible as the warm sunlight that bathed her shoulders and the ripple of the cool water across her breasts. He was strong and forceful and dynamic—and he was fun. And she wanted him as she had never wanted anyone in her life.

He wasn't holding her that close. Surprisingly, there was still space between them, and yet she was aware of just how mutual the wanting was, how great the need that pulsed through every sinew of his hard, virile body.

'Alex…'

It was a protest and a plea. But which one should he ignore?

As if he had a choice! Alex thought, wrestling with his over-taxed libido and his conscience. He could seduce her now, as easily and as effortlessly as every other woman he had ever taken to his bed, give her the pleasure she was begging for and ease the throbbing torture that had been his constant bedfellow ever since she had stumbled—unaware and unintentionally—back into his life two weeks ago. But the fact remained that, had she been aware of what she was doing, she wouldn't have come within a hundred-mile radius of him, let alone allow him to seduce her into his bed!

'You aren't ready for this.' It took every gram of his iron-clad will to drag the words past his throat. Colour suffused the skin across his hard-boned cheeks as he gazed down on the perfect beauty of her features. She looked tense, flushed, and absurdly disappointed, her face pained from some deep inner conflict of her own. 'We neither of us are,' he breathed raggedly, knowing even as he said it that—where he was concerned at any rate—it was a lie. 'Have your swim,' he advised curtly, pulling himself up out of the pool, because that was the only way he could handle it. 'But remember we have to leave here in forty-five minutes.'

* * *

There was a dress code on the island for dinner most nights in the best hotels. Sanchia recalled Alex telling her that before they had come away, and, just as she had expected, he took her to the best.

The very best, she realised, having gleaned from a brochure she had been reading on Bermuda during the past week that this one, on the western fringes of the island, with its pink cottage-style suites, its luxuriant manicured gardens and its five private beaches, was rated among the world's top ten hotels.

Now, in a short, simple red dress with fine straps and a low back that plunged almost to her waist, her thick glossy hair caught up in a softly rolled pleat, she felt a surge of warmth along her veins as she emerged from the powerful sports car Alex was opening for her and he dipped his head to murmur, 'You look absolutely stunning.'

It was the first compliment he had given her since leaving the house. Ever since that little incident in the pool he had seemed uncommunicative to the point of curtness.

'Thank you,' she breathed, hugging his compliment to her as she looked up into his hard, handsome face. 'So do you.'

In a silver-grey suit, white shirt and silver tie, he was drawing the eye of every woman coming in and out of the hotel. In fact, they complemented each other well, Sanchia thought, with a flush of pride to be accompanying him as she let him guide her through the scented grounds to the restaurant in the Colonial-style house. Her heart was singing in harmony with the song of the frogs and lizards concealed within every verdant bush and shrub.

'Do you let the house when you aren't staying here?' she asked, when they were seated in a dining room offering the ultimate in elegance: white table linen, soft lights and silver cutlery, hibiscus flowers decorating each table, vital splashes of colour against the pure damask.

'Only to friends and the odd business acquaintance,' he answered, studying the menu a waiter had brought them. 'There are very strict rules about foreign nationals letting properties in Bermuda. Besides, I like to fly out here every chance I can get, which I couldn't do if anyone else was in permanent residence.'

A few metres away a wall of glass had been slid back, giving onto a terrace where couples were enjoying pre-dinner cocktails overlooking the palm-fringed, gin-clear waters of what Alex had informed her earlier was Mangrove Bay.

Sanchia brought her attention back to the dynamic-looking man across the table, her pulse giving a sudden leap as her eyes rested, unnoticed for a few seconds, on his proud dark head, traced the strong contours of his face, the harsh outline of that intellectual brow, the high-boned cheek and forceful jaw. 'How long have you owned it?'

'Around two and a half years.' He brought his head up, his dark regard tugging over the soft oval of her face with its dewy skin and smoky-shadowed eyes, lingering with pulse-quickening deliberation, she felt, on the creamy fullness of her red lips. 'Negotiations for the place were already going through when—'

She glanced at him obliquely when he didn't finish. 'When what?' she prompted, interested.

'Nothing,' he said dismissively, then, with a sudden, heart-stopping smile, 'I'm afraid I'm in danger of boring you.' He glanced down again, surprising her with how abruptly he had changed the subject as he drew her attention to a dish on the menu.

'I don't normally like fish,' she replied obligingly. 'Well, not on plates.' She laughed. 'I much prefer to see them swimming around.'

'As per that host of little lodgers you keep in your flat?' Alex quipped dryly, referring to her tank of tropical fish, responsibility for which she had left in Jilly's capable hands.

'I could hardly look them in the gills if I'd been out tucking into one of their family, could I?' she admitted with a sheepish little smile, wondering if he thought her fickle, or crazy, or both, yet glad that their earlier tensions had all but evaporated now.

'Then I won't tell them if you don't,' Alex promised in laughing conspiracy. 'Try the Bermuda fish chowder with sherry peppers. It's delicious.'

It was. One of the country's national dishes, it was rich and spicy and full of flavour, and left her tongue zinging from the hot peppers.

'Is this a precedent for the holiday? Making me do things against my better judgement?' she asked in mock disapproval, as one of the impeccably dressed waiters whisked their emptied bowls away.

'Could anyone do that, Sanchia?'

He was serious suddenly, she realised, frowning.

'No, I don't think so,' she said, meeting his dark, disturbing gaze, wondering why he had asked.

Their main course was brought, their glasses were refilled, their desserts and cheeses accompanied by wines that complemented each to perfection.

'You certainly know how to live,' she complimented him when they were finishing what had to be the best meal she had ever tasted. The most enjoyable too, she thought, realising it was because of who she was with. 'This place is paradise!'

'Because its people appreciate and take care of what they have—and it isn't just sea, sun and sand. With little crime, rules like one car per family and a twenty-two-mile-an-hour speed limit, it means that fear and noise and danger don't prevail on the streets. Bermuda looks after its environment, its ecology, and its people. It's also very proud and fiercely protective of its traditional values.'

As he was proud, Sanchia thought, drawn by his formidable attraction, by the powerful aura of sexuality surrounding him. Proud of his self-sufficiency. His unquestionable professionalism. His own values.

'You love it, don't you?' she remarked, smiling, already understanding why.

His mouth turned wry, his irises darkening with some distant, inscrutable emotion. 'Some of my fondest memories are of this island.'

His words caused Sanchia's brow to furrow. She didn't have any memories, fond or otherwise—not since her teenage years anyway, she thought with a small sigh of frustration. The sound was lost beneath the soft strains of an acoustic guitar that had struck up a melody while they had been eating dessert.

'Shall we dance?' Alex invited, aware.

Her spirits returning easily, she smiled up at him, because he was already rising to his feet.

'You dance too?' She didn't have to add that she had been thinking all night how devastatingly handsome he was, and how that deep rich voice touched her senses in a way she was certain no other man's had ever done. How she had been clinging to his every perfectly enunciated word as if it were some kind of exotic music to her ears. He had to know that. How could he not? she wondered, despairing of herself.

He laughed, obviously used to feminine appreciation. 'Among other things,' he drawled suggestively, taking her hand and leading her over to the little area of dance floor in front of the guitarist.

Her body tensed as his arms went around her, every one of her senses seeming to step up a gear.

'We fit together very well, don't you think?' he murmured, his voice husky, his breath fanning the sensitive recess of her ear.

A deliciously erotic shudder ran along Sanchia's spine. Stiffening, she said thickly, 'You made me a promise.'

'About not telling the fish?' There was laughter in his voice again.

'You know what I mean,' she reminded him, weak from his nearness.

'Ah…' he breathed, as though his previous commitment about not slaking his lust was a different matter entirely.

'Alex!' Excitement burned with a warning in her bright, almond-shaped eyes.

'Then don't look at me like that,' he reprimanded softly.

'Like what?'

'With that provocative glitter in those seductive amber irises and temptation in that lovely mouth—or I might not be responsible for my actions.'

'I'm not.' The little croak escaped from a mouth that felt decidedly dry, and hot impulses leapt through her as he suddenly pulled her close.

'Yes, you are,' he countered, still in that softly reproving tone. 'And it's very difficult, knowing that I'd only have to kiss you for you to become a mass of sobbing sensuality in my arms.'

'No, I wouldn't,' she lied, wondering if he could feel the tension in her, the way her body trembled as his hard thighs brushed hers, so that she hardly dared breathe in case the action gave away just how he was affecting her.

'Do you want proof?'

His body was hard and warm beneath the expensive tailoring of his suit, his sleek appearance only masking the ruthless potency of the barely restrained male animal that lurked beneath.

'No,' she warned breathlessly, knowing he would be dangerous to provoke.

'A pity,' he breathed, turning her around in the soft light. 'I was really going to enjoy taking you up on the challenge.'

He was moulding her body to the strong hard lines of his, so that she was acutely aware of the warmth of his hand against her bare back and the disturbing contact of his hard abdomen pressing intimately against hers as they moved to the sensuously slow rhythm that was playing.

Sanchia's senses swam in a sea of heat and scent and texture. The feel of his suit against her bare legs, his intoxicating scent, the dangerous, excitingly hard edge of his masculinity...

Had she been here before? Been in his arms like this before? Was it only the wine and the music and the heady torture of being this close to him that was making her imagine he had made love to her after such a night as this? Because surely these feelings towards him that scared her with their intensity now, must have existed before? And it was obvious from what he had said about getting her into bed that the attraction was entirely mutual. And yet he wasn't admitting to having been her lover, was he? she reflected, her brain hurting as her speculation pulled her in all directions. He had even said in the pool that she wasn't ready for a relationship with him yet. Apart from which, if she had been that intimate with him in the past, there was no way, she was certain, that she would have forgotten...

Now, her senses saturated with the feel and sound and scent of him, and with every nerve trembling from the need to know, tentatively she whispered, 'Why—why did we break up?'

Alex's eyes when he lifted his head were screened by the heavy fringes of his lashes. How could he answer that? he wondered, feeling mercilessly challenged. How could he even begin to tell her the truth when the truth would only serve to rip them apart again?

Turning the hand he was holding in his, he lowered his mouth to the throbbing vein in her wrist, felt her instinctive withdrawal.

He was a stranger to her, he realised. Even so, he recognised the glaring sexual tension that held her in thrall, and a rush of hot desire flooded his loins.

'I've often asked myself that same question,' he responded heavily.

Her gaze darting to his, Sanchia tried to absorb his words, to think clearly above the devastating effects of what he was doing to her.

'You—you said it ran its course.'

'Did I?'

That we hadn't ever made love!

'I must have been mistaken, mustn't I?'

What was he saying? For a moment as she stared at his dark lowered head—felt the soft graze of his teeth across her wildly leaping pulse—she thought he had read her mind. Until she realised he was only referring to what she had said about their relationship running its course.

'And there were no regrets on either side?'

He straightened, half-shielded eyes scanning her ravaged

features with brutal sagacity. 'Are you saying you wish we hadn't, Sanchia?'

His face was suffused with heightened colour. Frustration, she suspected, with every instinct she possessed warning her to back away. But his thumb was arousing as it played over her wrist— still moist from his tongue's erotic assault—and the intensity of the desire she saw in those smouldering grey eyes seemed to be drugging her with its potency.

Involuntarily, her lips parted, her breasts straining from the urge to press herself against him, her whole body aching with need. He was going to kiss her and there wasn't a thing she could do to stop him. Didn't want to stop him! But then something made him glance up, over her shoulder, and she caught the expletive he uttered under his breath.

'Let's get out of here.' Already he was turning her in the direction of the exit.

'But my bag—'

'I'll get it,' he informed her abruptly. 'Wait for me outside.'

No further explanation or apology for cutting their evening short, Sanchia noted, when the taxi was carrying them back along lanes hemmed by shadowy hedges of hibiscus and heavily perfumed oleander flowers, each seeming to pulse with shrill sound now that the song of the frogs and lizards was at its height.

Was he that eager to be alone with her? she wondered, her pulses throbbing. If he was, and he intended to take her to bed, then she didn't know how she could prevent it. Whether she *wanted* to prevent it!

The house was quiet when they stepped inside, and she went stiffly ahead of him through the hall, realising, as she turned round at the foot of the stairs, that he was right behind her.

His face was slashed with shadows from a full high moon. He hadn't even bothered putting on the light.

'Alex…' She didn't know what she was going to say. Her heart was thumping wildly beneath the alluring little dress.

'Such conflict.' His words were soft and deep, laced with the harder edge of derision. 'Do you think I don't know how much you're fighting me under all that promise of seduction?' He laughed then, without humour, and stooped to press his lips to the throbbing pulse at her temple. 'Get a good night's sleep,' he advised her tightly. 'We've got a busy day tomorrow.' And he walked away, leaving her standing there chiding herself for feeling so ridiculously abandoned.

CHAPTER SIX

THE FOLLOWING DAY Alex took her across to Hamilton in his speedboat, to meet his friends, Chet and Hilary Tuxford, whose invitation included a barbecue lunch at their harbourside home.

'Alex has asked me to have a chat with you,' the psychiatrist remarked when Sanchia was helping her carry bowls of salad and dressings out to the table that had already been laid on their sun-drenched terrace. At fifty-something, Hilary Tuxford had taken early retirement and moved from England with her husband, a retired judge. She was a down-to-earth, bluntly spoken brunette, with sincere blue eyes and a friendly smile that endeared her to Sanchia in spite of her brusque, matter-of-fact manner. 'He said you've lost quite a vital chunk of your memory.'

Sanchia nodded, glancing down to the mooring, where the speedboat lay next to the Tuxfords' sailboat. Across the sparkling waters of the harbour the capital presented a picture of modern and Colonial architecture, white-roofed buildings in pastel shades of yellow, pink and blue.

Alex was standing by his craft, looking tall and muscular in white T-shirt and dark shorts beside the similarly-dressed, rather rounded figure of the older man. They were discussing some point of law, if the snippets of their conversation carried over to her on the warm breeze were anything to go by. But then Alex looked up, saw her standing there on the terrace, hair tumbling over one shoulder, the floaty white skirt she had teamed with a blue sun top moving softly in the wind, watching him. His eyes were too keen—too uncomfortably aware—and she turned quickly away.

'The consultant I saw in Ireland said it was rare for it not to have come back. That perhaps I didn't want it to.'

'As though you're blanking out some particular episode in your life?'

Sanchia turned and followed her hostess back into the house. 'Possibly.'

The woman handed her a large pepper mill, reached across for another containing salt. 'Alex told me you'd discharged yourself from your treatment sessions.' She gave the second mill to Sanchia and pushed back the sleeve of the shirt she wore over khaki Bermuda shorts. 'What sort of therapy have you undergone?'

When Sanchia told her, Hilary nodded contemplatively. 'There's certainly been nothing lacking in your treatment. It so happens I know one of the consultants who treated you, and he's regarded as being among one of the best in his field. I know you don't want to hear it from me as well, Sanchia, but the type of amnesia you're suffering *is* very rare. I've never handled a case quite like it in the whole of my career, and I can't promise that there's going to be any miracle cure. But that doesn't mean I won't try to help you if I can—even if it's only to lend support or provide a listening ear whenever you care to call. In fact, it will be nice having you around. When Chet and Alex get together I'm afraid I take a back seat to all that legal brilliance. Alex, as you're probably aware, is awesome.'

Sanchia laughed, watching her hostess take glasses from a cupboard. 'I know. He's terrifying.'

'Does he terrify you?' Four glasses in her arms, Hilary was the doctor again, all formality and probing intent.

'Perhaps that's the wrong word,' Sanchia murmured thoughtfully. 'Self-sufficient. Charismatic. Formidable.' Helplessly she shook her head, only able to echo exactly what Hilary herself had said to describe Alex Sabre. 'Awesome!' she echoed, laughing, unaware of the quiver in her voice and the hint of colour that animated her face.

'He's swept you off your feet,' the psychiatrist remarked.

Disconcerted by the woman's directness, Sanchia laughed again. 'That's a rather old-fashioned phrase.'

With the glasses on a tray, Hilary retrieved a bowl of delicious-looking ruby punch from the fridge. 'I can't think of a better way of putting it. And I can tell from the way you're blushing that you haven't slept with him yet.' There was nothing personal or particularly prying about Hilary's statement—nothing behind it but a generous willingness to help. 'So how did he manage to talk you into coming to Bermuda after just a couple of weeks' acquaintance?'

'Because he said I needed a holiday—and that there was a chance that you might be able to help me.'

'Ah…' Hilary breathed, as though something had just become clear to her.

'Apart from which,' Sanchia added, pulling a wry face, 'you probably know how forceful he can be.'

'And you're in love with him.'

Sanchia stopped dead in her tracks as they reached the patio doors opening onto the terrace. A mouthwatering aroma drifted in with the smoke from the various meats and seafood sizzling on the barbecue.

'No.' A troubled groove deepened between finely arched eyebrows. Was she? 'I don't know. I…'

'Oh, come on! No need to be bashful about it. Be honest with yourself. That's probably the first step to effecting a cure—facing up to the things you feel afraid of.'

'But I hardly know him!' Sanchia stressed quietly from the doorway as Hilary moved back outside again, afraid that their conversation might filter down to Alex—that he would overhear. 'And I certainly don't remember anything like that happening between us in the past.'

Setting the punchbowl down in the middle of the table, Hilary moved back to her. 'Apparently your psyche isn't too worried about that small consideration.'

'That's what scares me.'

'Is it?' Taking the mills from her, the woman paused in her task to study Sanchia's tense features with sharp, yet kindly assessing eyes. 'I would imagine that there's a lot more to it than that.'

Against the sudden deep boom of a horn from one of the cruise ships preparing to raise anchor in the harbour, Sanchia sent her hostess a guarded glance. 'Like what?'

'Oh…that you were in love with him before—whether he was aware of it or not—even whether you were.'

Hadn't she wondered that herself?

'But he said we hardly knew each other.'

Hilary gave her a sceptical look, took the mills over to the table and came back to her. 'You hardly know him now.'

Of course. And this clever woman had already sussed the extent of what Sanchia had thought were her closely concealed feelings for him.

'If it makes you feel any better, Sanchia,' she went on, 'I can only say I understand why. You're young. You're vulnerable. And, as you said, he is an incredibly charismatic man. You wouldn't be normal if you hadn't fallen for him hook, line and sinker—the moment he uttered his first words to you.'

'"Can I get you a drink?"'

About to step back into the house, the woman paused. 'What?'

'Those were the first words he said to me.'

The psychiatrist's scrutiny was keen. 'I thought you said you met in court.'

Sanchia shook her head. 'No. The first time.'

'How do you know?'

'What?'

'You said 'the first time'. I presume you meant…what was it?…two and a half years ago?'

Sanchia frowned. 'Did I?'

'How do you know what he said?'

Sanchia stared at the woman, her eyes wide and puzzled. 'I don't know.' She lifted a shaky hand to massage her forehead. Her head had started to ache. 'I just do.'

Hilary beckoned her inside, pushed her onto one of the stools in her state-of-the-art kitchen. 'Have you remembered that before?'

'No.' Apprehension showed in Sanchia's eyes, yet there was an underlying excitement in her voice as she said, 'Do you think it's coming back? Do you think my memory's actually returning?'

'I don't know, Sanchia. I wouldn't want to raise your hopes with false surmising. It might be something you imagined he said, or it might have actually happened. Where do you think you were at the time?'

Pained lines marked Sanchia's face as she struggled to recall, but the rewind button to her subconscious seemed to have stuck. 'I don't… Yes, I do!' Enthusiastically she jumped up. 'He said we were at a party!'

'*He* said.'

Of course. Her shoulders sagging, she clutched at one of the kitchen counters. That was what he had told her in the restaurant that first night he had taken her to dinner. It wasn't what she had remembered for herself after all.

'Don't get too dejected or disappointed, Sanchia,' Hilary advised, moving to open a cupboard and take out some plates. 'When—or if—your memory does come back, it's very likely to return in snatches. But there could be times when you might not be able to trust all you think you've remembered. It might be something you've dreamt, something you've heard someone else say…although of course if it's something you think Alex has said, you can always ask him.'

'Ask me what?'

Both women swung round on hearing the deep masculine drawl from the doorway. Neither had heard Alex come in.

A little frisson shot through Sanchia from the sheer impact

of his masculinity. He looked so vital, so devastatingly handsome, that for a moment any response she might have made stuck
in her throat.

'Nothing,' she said eventually, wondering what was preventing her from telling him. She didn't know, but something in her
rebelled against it. And what would it tell her if he *had* said that
anyway? she thought, justifying her reluctance. It was probably
the most popular chat-up line there was, so it was easy to imagine he might have said it.

'Don't be reticent about questioning him,' Hilary advised,
obviously mistaking Sanchia's reluctance for timidity. 'Interrogation isn't the sole prerogative of the advocates of this
world—brilliant and unorthodox though some of their tech-
niques may be.' This was said with a withering look at the tall
man who was leaning with arms folded against the metal
framework of the open doors.

'Meaning, Hilary?' A definite challenge laced the deep-
voiced question, and Sanchia's puzzled gaze flicked between the
two of them.

'Meaning that I know your methods, Alex, and that while I
admire the way you do things, I don't necessarily always approve
of them. A case like Sanchia's needs careful handling.'

With an easy grace he unfolded those powerful arms and
brought himself upright. 'You need to tell me that?'

'I've seen you in court.'

'And you think I might employ the same tactics to try and
wring her memory out of her?' He laughed rather harshly. 'She
isn't a witness for the prosecution.'

'Isn't she?'

Sanchia noticed the warning glance that Hilary sent him, and
the almost intimidating one he lobbed back in response.

What was Hilary suggesting? Sanchia wondered, puzzled.
That she and Alex were somehow involved in something that cast
them on opposite sides?

Whatever, there was definitely something going on between

the two of them, she decided during the tense little silence that followed, and was glad when Chet, striding up behind Alex, cut in with a cheery and unsuspecting, 'Well? Are we ready to eat?'

The punch was delicious, the hearts of palm that Hilary had prepared as a starter succulent and tender in their piquant dressing.

'Don't let Sanchia tell you she doesn't like fish,' Alex commented from across the table, noticing the way her eyes were roving over Chet's expertly barbecued wahoo steaks. 'She's a real little carnivore if she thinks there's nothing looking.'

They all laughed, Sanchia included.

'I'll get you for that!' she breathed, heady from the punch and the sensually-charged way in which he was looking at her.

'I'll look forward to it,' he drawled softly, ignoring the fact that Hilary Tuxford was sitting there regarding them both, weighing reactions, her doctor's cap very much in evidence. Nevertheless, his light-heartedness set the tone for the rest of the day.

'What did you think of them?' Alex shouted, to make himself heard above the buzz of the speedboat when they were cruising back across the wide, island-dotted waters of the Great Sound.

'I liked them very much,' Sanchia called back, shielding her eyes—despite her sunglasses—from the sun's low rays on the dazzling water.

He sent a glance in her direction. 'And was Hilary helpful?'

'As much as she could be.' Her sigh was lost beneath the growl of the powerful engine. 'She said pretty much the same as everyone else has, I'm afraid. I hope you're not too disappointed.'

'Disappointed?' He was looking at her curiously, his bronzed, beautifully tapered hands controlling the wheel.

'You're putting a lot of time and effort into helping me.'

'And you think that was the only reason I asked you here?' He sounded almost annoyed against the suddenly decreasing decibels of the motor.

As the boat burbled to a halt he turned her way, laying one strong bare forearm across the back of her seat. 'I brought you here because I wanted you with me,' he said firmly. 'Because Bermuda's a darn sight more fun with two—and because you looked as though you could do with a decent holiday. Your seeing Hilary was only a secondary consideration.'

Sanchia bit her lip. 'You mean the bait to get me here?'

He smiled seductively. 'That's right.'

Around them the sea was a deep and penetrating blue, pierced through with gold from the evening sun.

Unable to meet his eyes, Sanchia glanced over his shoulder, a treacherous excitement stealing through her as she regarded the familiar white roofs of the hotels and houses, the pastel-shaded cottages and the straggling trees that were a feature of the low-lying coast.

'She seemed almost cross with you earlier,' she reminded him, needing to steer the conversation away from their mutual and devastating attraction for each other.

'Cross?' Behind his dark glasses his eyes scanned her flushed yet puzzled features, his lips curling slightly, faintly amused.

'Challenging, then,' Sanchia corrected. 'She seemed to thoroughly disapprove of the way you do things, and yet to be totally in awe of your brilliance all at the same time. I felt she didn't know whether to scold or applaud you, and could only satisfy herself by doing both.'

He laughed softly, reaching out to catch a strand of her hair, damp and curling from the spray and the humidity.

'Just the medical mind in contest with the legal one, I'm afraid. The first time I met Hilary was when she was called onto a case I was defending to offer her professional opinion that one of the leading witnesses wasn't fit to give evidence. I argued that he was—and was proved right, as it turned out.'

'Naturally.'

The subtle lift of an eyebrow was his only response to her little riposte.

'Professionally,' he said, his mouth twitching in amusement, 'I think that still grates.'

'And you won the case.' Which went without saying, she thought, when his silence merely confirmed it.

She imagined him in action, saw him not in the casual clothes he was wearing now, that revealed the power and fitness of his bare, bronzed limbs, but in wig and black gown, like the Prince of Darkness, all humanity and compassion gone—held in check by formidable self-discipline as he embarked on a strategy that would tear the unsuspecting to shreds. She shuddered just imagining how his calculated skill and merciless persistence would have blown the opposition's case apart.

'You're cold,' he observed, the brush of his hand over her bare shoulder nevertheless sending a flare of tense heat through her before he reached in the back for the throw-over shirt he had brought with him and hadn't bothered to put on. 'Here.'

There was something thrilling and intimate about borrowing his clothes, and Sanchia hugged the secret to her as he turned aside and started the engine, resuming their journey home.

'Morally, Hilary and I are on the same side,' Alex commented, reverting to their earlier conversation after he had brought the little craft alongside the jetty in their own inlet and was securing the boat with strong, dexterous hands. 'And that's about getting to the truth. But there are times when our interests and opinions naturally collide. It's honest, it's healthy, and it makes for exhilarating debate out of our professional arenas. She's blunt. She doesn't suffer fools and she certainly doesn't take any prisoners—as you've obviously noticed. She's also one of the warmest people I know.'

His affection for Hilary Tuxford was evident as they moved over the crescent of soft sand towards the house, the sun a massive red ball behind them now, daubing its pale walls and drenching the fertile garden in crimson fire.

In the absence of a family, and apart from a couple of old university friends he had mentioned, Sanchia guessed that he was very much a loner, which made his relationship with the older couple particularly special, she felt, with a sudden aching desire to fill the void.

'Were you close to your parents?' she enquired, her heart giving a little leap as he reached for her hand.

'I was close to my mother,' he answered, 'but she died when I was ten years old.'

'How awful!' She hadn't realised it had happened while he was still so young. 'How did you manage? You and your father?'

After the briefest hesitation, he said, 'My father was married to someone else.'

Coming up through a rash of flame-tinged yucca plants, she glanced up at his dark profile. 'They were divorced?'

'No.' He let go of her hand because the path was too narrow to accommodate the two of them. 'He was already married to someone else when my mother met him—fell in love with him.' From just behind her his voice had taken on a decidedly harder edge. 'After Mother died he took me in, and my stepmother never let him—or me—forget it.'

'That's dreadful!' Some creature whistled softly through the shrubbery ahead of them, though it was too early yet for the nightly reptilian chorus.

'Not really. She had her own child, still a babe in arms.'

His half-brother, she remembered, whom he'd said had played too near the edge. Sympathetically, she recalled how tragically he had died.

'Were you close to your brother?'

The path had widened, but he didn't reach for her hand again. She was surprised by how much she wanted him to.

'No.' His response was flat and decisive. 'I never really had the chance to be. I was away at school and then university most of the time he was growing up. We had different tastes—different values. And then for the last few months of his life we were estranged.'

'I'm sorry,' Sanchia murmured and, guessing that the raw edge to his voice had to be regret, added, 'Do you want to talk about him?'

Dear Lord! She didn't know what she was asking! Alex's teeth ground together so tightly that his jaw locked as though in a painful vice. 'No,' he said thickly at length.

She was finding it difficult now, keeping up with his powerful stride. 'Sometimes,' she suggested, 'it helps to unburden yourself on a friend.'

'I said no, Sanchia!'

His words came back like a whip across her face, jerking her head back as though he had actually struck her.

Gone was the warm and teasing companion he had been all day. In his place was a cold and shuttered wall of masculinity. His features were rigid with a tension so palpable she wanted to reach up and touch it, draw gentle fingers down his face and soothe away whatever was making him look so bleak.

Ask him, the psychiatrist had advised of the things Sanchia wanted to know. *Don't be intimidated by him*, she had implied. But there were times, like now, when he seemed so distant and unapproachable—in fact, whenever she tried to get him to talk about his family. She had only been making conversation, trying to get to know more about him!

But what did it matter if he didn't want to open up and talk about himself? It wasn't any of her business anyway.

She was looking very hurt, Alex thought, glancing round because she had dropped back, letting him go on ahead. Her hair was wild and wet from being on the boat, and his shirt hung provocatively open over her low-cut camisole, emphasising her femininity in a way that made him want to rip off the unflattering garment and embark on a slow and pleasurable passage of seduction.

'And now I've upset you,' he said, having waited for her to catch up, noticing how her mouth was set in a wounded yet alluring little pout.

'No, you haven't.' But she kept on walking.

'Then why are you sulking?' he challenged, following her.

'I'm not sulking.'

'Yes, you are.' With one easy stride he reached forward and grabbed her wrist. A shocked little cry left her as he pulled her round, hauling her into his arms. 'Do you know what I do with young women who sulk?'

She didn't, but dangerous impulses leapt through her when she realised she was going to find out.

'Alex, please,' she protested, her mind rejecting the arms that were tightening around her as much as her body craved them. And, as if he knew the conflict that was raging inside her, he took the decision into his own hands, blotting out all her objections beneath the hard domination of his mouth.

Her hands came up to clutch at his shoulders, her head tipping back as his kiss deepened, leaving no room for objection as her body turned traitor on her, producing a small groan of need when his arm slid down over her soft skirt to pull her hips hard against the superior strength of his.

The softness of his clothes couldn't conceal how much he wanted her. She could feel the hardness of his arousal pressing against her. Her breasts ached in response, flowering against his palm in response to the hand that had pushed aside his shirt. Its massaging warmth through the ineffectual barrier of her camisole was threatening to drive her delirious.

When the kiss had ended he clasped her hard against his rigid masculinity, his jaw against her temple, his body throbbing, one hand caressing the soft, sultry dampness of her hair.

Sanchia.

He scarcely dared breathe her name, afraid that his voice would convey the depth of his agonising need, afraid one mistake on his part—one move too soon—would drive her away from him.

He wanted to tell her everything. Perhaps Hilary had been right to upbraid him almost openly for not doing so. He grimaced, clenching his teeth against the fever of wanting that was consuming him. But the psychiatrist didn't have his memories any more than he himself could claim the luxury of oblivion—which, ironically, made him envy Sanchia.

He wanted her to remember him. To carry her back to the house and make love to her without reservation, without this waiting, without this killing need for restraint. To hear her soft, rapturous moans as he entered her, pleasured her, filled her with his body and soul—but without the dark days of the past intruding on what they could offer each other.

Pressed so close to him, Sanchia heard the breath that shivered through his lungs, could have sworn she felt his strong body tremble. But then he sighed deeply, releasing her.

'I have to go out,' he surprised her by saying. 'There are one or two people I've agreed to see while I'm here. Do you think you can amuse yourself while I'm gone?'

If his words disappointed her, then Sanchia was determined not to let it show.

'Of course,' she murmured as they reached the house, and twenty minutes later, freshly showered and looking dynamic in a pale shirt and dark trousers, he left.

The following days were filled with the fun that Alex had promised. He taught her to wind-surf and water-ski off their own private beach, showed her the best places to snorkel so that she could observe the striped and brightly coloured fish darting in and out of the coral, and he actually seemed interested when she talked to him about camera exposures and tricks of light and other expertly acquired secrets of professional photography. On top of all that, he was exhilarating to talk to, too. Fascinating, exciting, and extremely knowledgeable.

'How come you know so much?' she laughed one afternoon, after he had driven her to a small cove on the island's South Shore and they had covered everything from Mozart to Bermudian politics.

'Put it down to experience,' he told her, far too modestly. 'Although I was once accused by my teachers of having a brain like a sponge.'

'What? Full of holes?' Sanchia teased.

Seeing the challenge in his eyes, she ran shrieking away from him, paying for it when he chased her through an arch of spectacular rock before bringing her down with him on the soft sand.

She let out a small cry as he turned her over, holding her there, face down across his knees.

'You were saying?' Hand raised, he was laughing, waiting for her to repeat it.

'You heartless brute!' she accused breathlessly as red-hot sensations tore through her. Contrarily, she felt the burn of stinging tears behind her eyes.

He laughed again, and rolled her round, so that her bikini-clad body was effectively trapped between his bare chest and his hard warm thighs.

'Not really,' he whispered hotly against her mouth.

Black lashes fanned across his cheeks as his eyes lowered to question the tell-tale glitter in hers, and very gently then he bent his head and touched his tongue to her lips.

His kiss, which had begun as a mere tasting of her mouth, deepened into something much more complex and demanding, bringing her straining against him, welcoming the warm hands that slid possessively around her bare midriff, not caring that there were other people on the beach.

'You're an exhibitionist,' she breathed when she could speak again, tasting the salty velvet of his shoulder beneath her swollen mouth. 'You love an audience. That's why you're such a damn good barrister.'

'And that excites you,' he murmured, aware.

This time as his mouth covered hers she felt the full elemental force of his desire. Hers flared to life beneath it, strangling her reason, her judgment and her thinking, until somehow she found the strength to push him away.

'Why do you fight me,' he queried softly, granting her freedom, 'when every message I get from you tells me the opposite?'

'It's too complicated,' she said, moving away from him. 'Much too complicated—oh!' Her hair moved wildly as she shook her head in an effort to jolt what had suddenly seemed to surface from her long-buried memory.

'What is it?' Alex demanded, seeing her staggering. He leapt up, still aroused, though his face was almost ashen. 'What's wrong?'

'I don't know. I—' Slender fingers clutched her temple and she met his gaze, her eyes turning fearfully from his harsh and penetrating regard. 'Oh, Alex! Why are you looking at me like that?'

'What are you remembering?' he rasped, his fingers bruising on her upper arms as he urged her back into the seclusion of the rocks, where they couldn't be seen. 'You remembered something, didn't you? *Didn't you*?'

'I don't know!'

'Yes, you do! You were reminded of something. What was it?'

'I don't know! It was just something…something I thought you said.'

'Something *I* said?'

'I don't know!' Her features were pained from the effort of concentrating as the pressure increased on her fine bones.

'Think, Sanchia! Think!'

'I can't! Oh, Alex, please! Don't make me go there!' It was like a repeat performance of the night when he had shown her that photograph, when he had seemed to offer her a key to unlock her mind which she had been too afraid to turn.

'Why not?' he challenged roughly. 'Is it so terrible?'

'Yes!'

'Why? How do you know if you can't even remember?'

'I don't know how!' She was near to tears. 'I just do!'

His face blazed with anger, or maybe it was simply frustration. 'You've got to face it, Sanchia. Sooner or later you've just got to face it. They're only memories. How can they hurt you?'

'I don't know!'

'Yes, you do. But you won't even admit that! You're a coward, Sanchia!'

'Stop it!'

'A first-rate coward!'

'Leave me alone! I can't stand this!' She was pummelling his shoulders, meeting a hard, resistant wall that was inexorable and unyielding. 'I can't! Stop it! Stop interrogating me!'

As if her words had triggered something in that keen mind, his deep chest lifted and he drew her close, uttering a self-loathing oath against her hair.

'I'm sorry. Hilary advised me to handle you with kid gloves, and here I am treating you like some hardened criminal,' he apologized, exhaling heavily.

Only a hardened criminal wouldn't know the pleasure of his arms after he had stripped them bare, Sanchia thought, drowning in his naked warmth. Or this excruciating tenderness that was the flipside of his honey-tongued brutality.

'Perhaps you've been mixing with the wrong type of company too long,' she chided softly, trembling from the sensations he was arousing in her again.

'Perhaps,' he murmured, with a smile in his voice now. 'All I know right at this minute is that I want to make love to you, Sanchia. And that if we go back to the house there will be nothing to stop me doing what I've wanted to do since I saw you again in that court and taking you straight up to bed. Undressing you. Loving you...'

His words were a turn-on in themselves, causing her eyes to close, her lips to tilt with unrestrained and involuntary provocation to his.

'No, Sanchia,' he breathed, a hair's breadth from her mouth, yet she felt the tremor that shook his hardened, virile body. 'I'd just be doing something you might well end up hating me for in time, much as I want to avail myself of all you're offering.'

She felt ashamed then, and the eyes she opened to his were bewildered, humiliated, hurting.

'You're brutally honest.'

'No, not brutal,' he said. 'And not particularly honest.'

Hair dark as polished jet cascaded over her shoulder as she tilted her head, her expression guarded. 'Why not?'

'Because if I were I'd remind you that you once called me a single-minded, arrogant bigot.'

She uttered a tremulous little laugh. 'I called you that?'

He grimaced. 'I probably deserved it.'

'Why? What did you do?'

Behind them a gull shrieked, swooping low over the ancient rocks as they had been doing for centuries.

'It was probably more what I *didn't* do,' Alex said with a self-derisive pull of his mouth.

Sanchia's eyes were puzzled. 'I don't understand.'

'No,' he said with a sigh. 'Neither do I.'

Fine brows drawing closer together, she said, 'You aren't making sense.'

He held her away from him, studying her at arm's length, his masculine gaze absorbing every feature of her soft, bewitching face and her enchanting figure, with its full, voluptuous breasts, the narrow waist and smooth rounded hips that could cradle a man all the way to heaven.

'We didn't have very much going for us, Sanchia. That's the truth of it.' Not then, he thought. Not the first time around. But if the gods would just give him this chance, with the help of hind-sight—now that he was wiser—he could control the situation...

'And if I were brutally honest, my lovely girl,' he said, 'you'd know it, and you wouldn't particularly thank me for it.'

Which told her nothing, she thought, baffled, before he tugged her by the hand, saying, 'I'm going for a swim. Come on. I think we both need cooling off, don't you?'

CHAPTER SEVEN

HILARY TUXFORD had said that if Sanchia's memory returned it might do so in snatches, but there had been no more snippets of long-forgotten phrases or words spoken, not the slightest glimpse of anything in her lost past.

A couple of days later they met Chet and Hilary in Hamilton. The Bermudian capital was alive with tourists, so they were lucky to find a table for lunch in one of the colourful historic buildings that lined its main street.

'Are there any developments you'd like to bring to my attention?' the psychiatrist asked Sanchia when they were settled—inside, because the balconies were full—sipping long cool appetisers before their meal.

'Nothing,' Sanchia admitted with a rather weary shrug, her attention drawn by the clip-clop of hooves to the street outside, where one of the horse-drawn carriages available for hire to tourists was making its way along the busy thoroughfare.

'Nothing,' Alex echoed beside her, 'because every time she gets close to remembering something she backs away. Now, why do you think that is, my clever learned friend, with your far greater experience and wisdom than mine?'

'Is it greater, Alex?' Hilary's tone was contesting. 'I'm sure you can unlock her if no one else can. She must be quite a challenge for you. And I know how much that brilliant mind of yours thrives on challenges.'

'What would you have me do?' he said dryly, his fingers long and dark against the cool condensation of his glass. 'Feed her to the wolves and see what's destroyed first—her sanity or her future?'

The pyschiatrist's mouth firmed as she took his castigation on the chin. 'I'm pleased to hear you're concerned about both.'

The two great minds were locked in combat again, and, looking exasperatedly from one to the other, Sanchia couldn't help chipping in—primarily to Alex. 'Would you please stop talking about me as though I'm not here?'

'I'm sorry, Sanchia.' Contrition marked Hilary's swift response. 'Forgive us for forgetting our manners. I'm afraid I've always been too outspoken for my own good, and Alex is a master at making one say more than one intends—as I'm sure you've realised by now.'

Apart from which, it stimulated the psychiatrist to argue with him, Sanchia decided. From the woman's flushed cheeks and her bright, animated eyes, it was clear that even the mature, practical Hilary wasn't immune to this man's lethal magnetism and charisma.

'What have you been doing with yourself since we saw you last?' It was Chet who spoke, taking the tension out of the moment with the well-timed and rather banal question he directed at Sanchia. 'Alex tells me you've had a trip out this morning in the glass-bottomed boat?'

'Yes.' She returned his rather avuncular smile. But she didn't tell this kindly man that it had happened again, when she had been on deck photographing the harbour—that feeling of *déjà vu* as she'd moved her camera round and caught Alex looking at her through the lens. Startled, stunned by the intensity of the feeling, she'd said nothing, just stood there staring at him over her lowered camera. He hadn't made any comment either, but she knew he'd been aware of it. He must have been, she thought, and wondered, as she glanced at his starkly handsome profile and felt her heart give a lurch, if everything he did where she was concerned wasn't all part of some carefully calculated plan.

She was glad of the change of subject, however, and the next ten minutes were spent discussing the new dockyard and the age-old topic of the country's independence, until Hilary announced casually, 'I hear storms are forecast. I'm not surprised. We expect it to be hot at this time of the year, but the heat this month's been relentless. By the way, Alex, I don't know whether you're aware of it or not…' On his other side, she leaned closer to him, her tone dropping confidentially, but not so much that Sanchia couldn't make out what was being said. 'Yasmin Croft's back in Bermuda. The whole family are here for the summer.'

A nerve seemed to flicker in the tough masculine jaw, and Sanchia could almost sense the curious tension bouncing off his hard, powerful body. 'Yes, I saw Danny the first evening we arrived.' His smile was fleeting, though his tone and manner were casual enough as he added, 'Thanks for letting me know,' before turning away.

'I understand you're rather fond of badminton?' Chet caught Sanchia's attention with his unexpected remark, unaware of her sudden inexplicable uneasiness, for which she could see no reason, unless it was because of the dark absorption of Alex's cool grey eyes. 'Perhaps while you're here you'd like to give me a game. Hilary doesn't play, and it's far too tame, of course, for Alex. He prefers the cut and thrust of something much more energetic and opponent-crushing, like squash.'

Well, he would, Sanchia thought, a picture flashing through her mind of Alex in white sports gear, having just finished a punishing game, his sweat-soaked shirt almost transparent across his powerful chest, his shorts a stark contrast against dark, hair-roughened thighs. She could almost smell the masculine scent of his hard, victorious body, feel the pulsing warmth of him burning against her as he made a conquest of her in an entirely different way.

Was it feeling as she did about him that was making her imagination run riot? she wondered, shaken. Or was she remembering something? Had she known what it was like to be driven delirious in this man's bed, to be a willing slave to her own ensnared sexuality?

No!

The perspiration she could feel dampening her skin was very real, and her head was pounding. Vaguely she was aware of the waiter coming up and asking Alex if he would care to choose the lobster he had ordered for his main course.

The lobsters were in the glass tank she could see in the middle of the restaurant: still moving; very much alive, oblivious to their fate.

'No! You can't!' It came out like the plea of a tortured child. Her blood seemed to be gushing in her ears.

'What is it, Sanchia?' Alex's voice sounded real and close through a haze of spinning unreality—very calm, remarkably controlled.

'It's so hot in here. Perhaps that's the trouble.' It was Hilary speaking this time. 'I'm surprised they don't do something with the air-conditioning.' She leaned towards Alex again, said something that Sanchia didn't catch.

'Is everything all right, sir?' the young waiter asked, addressing Alex, obviously assessing him to be the dominant member of the group.

'Yes. Everything's fine, thank you,' he said, urbanely enough, but there was an authoritative dismissal in the deep tones. As the waiter left them to it, Sanchia noticed the challenging glance Alex exchanged with the other woman. 'Save it, Hil,' he advised thickly, getting up. Already he was beside Sanchia, pulling out her chair. 'Come on.' His voice was soft, the hand under her elbow warm and firm and controlling. 'I'm taking Sanchia home.'

The humidity outside was almost choking.

'Here,' Alex directed, handing her into a taxi that materialised for him at the kerbside at the snap of his fingers, reminding her that they had caught the ferry to Hamilton that morning, leaving the car at the house.

'What a crass thing to do! What will Chet and Hilary think of me?' she wailed, sinking back against the soft leather. The air in the taxi as it pulled away was blessedly cool. 'I don't know what came over me. I acted like a prize fool back there.'

'You acted like a grown woman who was simply overcome by heat and circumstances,' Alex answered, mercifully understanding.

The smile she sent him was weary. 'You're far too kind.'

That hard mouth pulled down one side. 'Is that what you think?'

'Sorry, I forgot. You aren't, are you?' A wry warmth lit her eyes now that she was beginning to feel better. 'Keep telling me that and I'll start to believe it.'

He made a self-deprecating sound down his nostrils. 'You'd probably be well advised to, Sanchia.'

But the arm that slid around her shoulders was excruciatingly tender, and she let her head fall back against the soft cotton covering his shoulder as though it were second nature to her to do so.

The scent of jasmine impinged on her nostrils from an air-freshener plugged into the dashboard, together with Alex's very personal scent, mingling with that all too familiar cologne. His arm was strong and protective, his body warm and solid, and, leaning against him like this, she felt her own inner strength reinforced in a way that she could never have dreamed possible. He threatened her equilibrium; intimidated her with his daunting mind and his forceful character; yet he excited her too, stirring her senses and evoking physical responses from her in a way that made her feel exhilarated, happy, alive.

I love you!

She turned her face into his hard warmth, wondering how she could acknowledge it so easily. Had she loved him before, as Hilary suggested? Had he rejected her love? Failed to recognise it? Or had this emotion been generated only in meeting him again?

'You said heat and circumstances just now...' Her voice faltered as she reminded him, because how could she be this close to him—feel like this—without his realising the extent of her emotions?

'Did I?' When he didn't expand, she lifted her head and met eyes that were so profoundly searching in their intensity—so penetratingly dark—that her limbs went weak.

'What circumstances?' she enquired, her voice cracking, her mouth suddenly dry.

'Whatever was making you look so lost—so haunted—back there. Do you want to talk about it?' His voice was coaxing, silkily caressing in its persuasiveness.

About what? About imagining you peeling off your sportswear and making love to me?

'There's nothing to talk about,' she said, her temples throbbing from those starkly sensual images that still made her blood race through her—because how could she tell him that?

A glance upwards again showed her the clean thrust of his jaw and the taut lines of his profile as he gazed—sightlessly, she sensed—at the colourful Colonial buildings, with their fluttering Union Jacks proclaiming the island's ties with Britain, and at the myriad red scooters lined up under a dark green canopy of trees.

'It was some sort of experiment, wasn't it?' she challenged.

Her statement brought his attention back to her. 'What was?'

'Today. Coming here in the first place. You're trying to do something together, aren't you? You and Hilary. Have you placed some sort of intellectual stake on which one of you can crack me first?'

His chest stirred with the soft laughter that rippled from his throat.

'No, we haven't,' he assured her, his tone gently reprimanding. 'And the last thing I see you as is an experiment, Sanchia.'

'No? Not just the smallest challenge to that restless intrepid brain of yours? The chance that I'll be so grateful to you if my memory does come back, I'll be falling over myself to sleep with you?'

'I don't want your gratitude,' he said tersely.

No, but he wanted her in his bed. Hadn't he already admitted that?

'And you have a very warped view of my motives,' he chided softly, 'if you think I'm only interested in you as a challenge to my intellectual ego, with a possible sexual bonus thrown in at the end of it all. Apart from which, the last thing I have in mind when I do get you into my bed, Sanchia, is to do any sleeping. Stay there,' he commanded in a low, firm voice, as his last disconcerting remark had her trying to put some distance between them.

She obeyed after a moment, and stayed with her head against his shoulder, outwardly quiescent though her blood was racing, listening to the heavy rhythm of his heart.

Over her head, his eyes dark and reflective, Alex gazed out at the activity in the street.

Smartly dressed Bermudians were going about their daily business, alongside the more casually dressed tourists from the two cruise ships at anchor in the harbour on the opposite side of the road. A woman in a brightly coloured sunhat drew his attention to the toddler in the buggy she was pushing, and from nowhere a shaft of pain lanced through him, so unexpectedly sharp it left him almost winded, aching for the child he had never held, never even got to see.

Beneath his arm he felt Sanchia tremble, reluctantly compliant yet silently resisting, deprived of that part of her past that made her enviably at peace in her ignorance.

He wanted to shake her out of it. Sink his fingers in her hair and squeeze her beautiful head until the memories came flooding out of her—squeeze until she remembered the ecstasy, the agony—him!

Share this with me! I need you to share this with me!

But she wasn't ready to, Alex realised with features bleak as a cliff-face, and knew that if he demanded that of her then she would only pull further away from him and retreat even deeper into herself.

They had dinner on the terrace that evening, brought out to them by Crystal, who quickly and discreetly retreated in between serving and clearing each course.

Now they were on their coffee, and though their conversation throughout the meal had been light and effortless, the underlying sexual tension that lay between them seemed to Sanchia to be building with each second that passed. It was there in the odd casual glance, in their free and easy laughter, and in those increasingly long moments of earth-shattering eye contact that left her weak and wanting as the sun sank into the sea and the moon rose silver over the white roof of the house.

'This place is fantastic,' she murmured after one such moment, using her surroundings as an excuse to break free from the dangerous pull of his magnetism, absorbing the serene lines of the boat bobbing beside the jetty, the pale curve of the beach lapped by a gentle sea. Hilary had forecast storms, she remembered, but they hadn't come. 'There isn't anywhere else I'd rather be right now.'

'Isn't there?' His eyes touched the golden slope of her bare shoulders, their heat as tangible as the warm wind against her skin as they slid with rousing sensuality down over the strapless white dress that hugged her slender figure, to the deep cleft between her generous breasts. 'I wish I could say the same thing.'

His meaning was clear enough, and Sanchia felt her breasts tighten in response. With his features hardened by the shadows, and his black hair contrasting starkly with the loose-fitting white shirt he wore, gleaming under the subdued lights around the terrace, he had never looked more attractive or more dynamic.

She wanted nothing so much as she wanted to end this night in the electrifying ecstasy of his arms—and it would be electrifying. She didn't need help to recognise that. But an element of doubt remained, along with the fear that if she did succumb to this reckless wanting that was becoming almost too much to contain, she wouldn't just be giving herself to him physically but emotionally as well. And something deep in her subconscious warned her that in that lay heartache of the most devastating kind.

'I think I'll go inside,' she announced breathlessly, getting up. 'Thank you for a lovely evening, Alex.'

'Running away from it, Sanchia?' His tone was softly mocking as he followed her example and rose to his feet, his chair an ominous scrape over the tiled floor.

'From what?' she parried, her tongue seeming to stick to the roof of her mouth.

'From what we both know is inevitable.'

'Don't be silly.' Her breasts were rising and falling a little too quickly. 'I'm tired, that's all.'

'Liar.'

'Alex, don't…' she murmured, fear making her eyes wary. He was moving over to her, intensely masculine in the loose shirt and the dark trousers that hugged his hard hips, his footsteps deceptively light over the terracotta tiles.

'Don't what?' he demanded. 'Kiss you? Embrace you? Put an end to this ridiculous pretence that is driving us both near insane? You want me as much as I want you, so why don't we just be honest with ourselves?'

Sanchia's breath seemed to catch in her lungs. 'And have an affair?'

Something gave a tug at the firm, masculine mouth. 'Not the word I'd use, but the outcome would be pretty much the same,' he admitted, his cool, sophisticated elegance just a smokescreen for the boiling cauldron of predatory emotions beneath.

If only she could! Sanchia thought. But she didn't have the courage—or the lack of sense—to embark on something so foolish when every instinct told her she would only wind up humiliated or hurt, or both, with a man like him.

Her ruby-tipped fingers trembled against the low-necked, scalloped-edged top that did very little to conceal her breasts. 'I don't go in for casual affairs.'

'Don't you?' His eyes were dark with desire, the smile that touched his lips so sensually provocative that Sanchia felt as though she were suffocating.

Was he questioning her morals? she wondered, stunned that he might think so. Or merely challenging her ability to know for sure?

'Turn around.'

A fine line appeared between her eyebrows, but with her heart leaping against her ribcage she did as she was told.

His cool fingers slid under the heavy silk of her hair and lifted the dark swathe, exposing the pale, vulnerable line of her neck to the galvanising warmth of his lips.

A shuddering sensation trembled along her spine, dragging the breath from her lungs as desire, both hot and sweet, pierced her loins, turning her insides to liquid from the aching need to be filled with him.

The pads of his fingers brushed her heated flesh as he let her hair fall to slip something around her neck.

She gasped as she gazed down at the cool metal lying against her skin. It was a delicate gold chain, holding the equally delicate and graceful gold image of a gull in flight. The island's national bird. A Bermudian long-tail.

She frowned, fingering the smooth surface of the metal, and its finer, sharper edges, pressing it to her chest as a fog of disturbing emotions descended over her. Had he—had someone—done something like this before? The line between her eyes deepened as she stared at the gift he had given her. But the little bird was giving nothing away.

'I saw you looking at these pendants in Hamilton today.' Strong hands on her shoulders were turning her round to face him.

She had been, but hadn't realised that he had noticed. When had he got it? she wondered. When she'd wandered off to buy some more film for her camera?

Her throat felt clogged with emotion. 'You shouldn't have.'

'Why not?' His tone dismissed the gesture as insignificant. 'Afraid I might be trying to buy my way into your bed?'

'Are you?' It was a tremulous challenge, soft against the dark velvet of the night.

A flash of anger lit his eyes and was swiftly banked behind some darker, inscrutable emotion.

'Could I?'

Sanchia held her breath at the raw desire in his voice, at the emotion that seemed to be drowning her in those grey eyes. 'No.'

'Because you want more than you think I could offer?'

He laughed softly then, the masculine fingers that splayed possessively across her breast causing her to tense, her lashes to droop under the keen gaze that was mercilessly assessing her reaction. He could feel the way her nipple hardened beneath the exquisitely sweet torture of his thumb, the way her breathing came far too fast. He wasn't stupid, she thought despairingly.

'I think you're very wise,' he said hoarsely, letting his hand fall. 'For both our sakes. I would hate for you to say at some later date that I took advantage of you. And that is, after all, my dearest, what I'd be doing.' His mouth on hers was gentle yet fleeting, leaving her tense and traitorous body aching for more. 'Goodnight, Sanchia. Sleep well.'

It was an agonising and irrational disappointment when he let her go.

She slept fitfully, waking at intervals in a tense fever of longing, unconsciously listening for any sound of movement in Alex's bedroom.

Where was he now? Asleep? Had he gone to bed the instant she had left him and fallen into a relaxed, untroubled slumber? Or was he lying in his room, just as she was, aching with frustration just from imagining what their lovemaking would be like?

Her breasts throbbed from the way he had touched her, her whole body burning for the feel of his hands until she thought she would scream with her need for him. But he had said that making love with her would only be taking advantage of her, that she would want more from him than he could possibly give. So in spite of all they had been doing together, all the laughter, their mutual interests and the rapport they seemed to share, it still wasn't enough to make him actually *care*.

She groaned, turning over in bed, hearing the wind picking up outside. A sudden flurry of rain changed quickly to a heavy tropical downpour, rattling the fronds of the palms outside her window and soaking the fertile earth.

Sunshine. Rainfall. Fertility. The words lodged in her tired brain like a mantra, until she fell into another restless sleep and dreamed she was scuba-diving in a giant fish tank with lobsters floating past. She swam in panic to the surface, and only when she had broken through it realised that it was frozen. It was sunny above the water, and a swan was emerging from out of the dark depths, splintering the ice, its huge white wings outstretched as it took off towards the light. She tried to get up and follow it, but something was dragging her back. She was back in the water, except now the dream had changed and it was the one she always dreamed, where she was wandering down a dark and lonely corridor from which there was no escape.

She was sobbing loudly and uncontrollably, and someone was shaking her gently by the shoulders.

'Wake up, Sanchia! It's all right. It's just a dream. Come on. Wake up,' a deep male voice was urging softly.

Sanchia's eyes flickered open.

'It's all right,' Alex whispered, his voice gently reassuring. In the shadowy room she could almost believe there was tenderness in his smile.

He was still dressed in the shirt and trousers he had been wearing earlier. His hair was ruffled, though, and his shirt was unbuttoned almost to the waist.

'What is it?' he pressed.

She was surprised to find herself sitting up in bed, held close against the hard wall of his chest.

'You're damp,' she murmured shakily, too conscious of his musky male scent, the crispness of his body hair against her cheek, exposed by his gaping shirt.

'I know. I've been out walking.'

Had he? Had she been right? Had frustration kept him from going to bed? she wondered, soothed and yet stimulated by his closeness, by his hard warmth and the hard steady pumping of his heart.

'I keep getting these dreams.' She began explaining to him, mindful of the fact that she was wearing nothing but a short re-

vealing nightie. 'The same dream. I'm running down a long corridor that never ends and I'm looking for something. There are
lots of doors on either side of me but I can't open any of them.
It's as though someone needs me. They're waiting at the end of
this long corridor, but I can never reach it. Never reach them!
And then it switches and I'm the one who's waiting. I'm waiting and waiting. But for what I don't know. It's a kind of apprehension—fear—and yet sometimes I feel happy too. And then
it's gone. Then it's like something's been wrenched from me—
but I don't know what—or what it is that I'm looking for. Oh,
Alex, help me! Do you think I'll ever find the answer to it? Do
you think I'll ever *know*?'

'If you really want to remember.' His breath came warm and
deeply against the top of her gleaming head. 'Perhaps your subconscious is trying to tell you something, but it won't come
back by forcing it. You must try to be patient.'

'That's what everyone's told me.' She glanced up at him,
gave him one of her weary little smiles. 'But still nothing ever
comes.'

'Perhaps there *is* someone who's missing you,' he supplied
gently. 'Have you ever considered that?'

She shook her head. 'No,' she dismissed on a little wry note.
'Not after having told everyone I was on my own and with a line
through *Next of Kin* in my passport.'

'Not a boyfriend or a lover?' he suggested casually, and when
she shook her head again said, 'How do you know?'

*Because I want you so much, and I know I've never felt this
way about anyone else!* her heart clamoured unequivocally. The
face upturned to his was harrowed as she whispered, 'I just do.'

Alex's breath came heavily through his nostrils. She looked
very young and very vulnerable, trusting yet guarded, a child, a
woman and a temptress—all rolled into one.

'You're over-tired,' he asserted, as if she *were* a child—because that was the only way he could keep his mind off the
temptress, and the fact that she was wearing so little it would

have taken no persuasion on his part to ease those thin straps down over her beautiful breasts and—

Feeling the tense stirring of his lower body, he slammed the lid down hard on his raging frustration. 'Try and get some rest,' he advised huskily, pressing her back against the pillows.

'Don't leave me.' It was an anxious appeal to him in the darkness. 'Stay with me.' Her slender hands were locked around his hard wrists. 'I don't want to be alone.'

Alex dragged another breath through his lungs. She had had a nightmare, and here he was abandoning her because he couldn't control his damn libido! He never had been able to where she was concerned—right from the first.

'I won't leave you,' he promised, his voice thickened by desire.

Lying down on the bed, he pulled her back against him, gritting his teeth against the sensations that assailed him as her warm slenderness shaped itself to his hard, aroused warmth. Because he *was* aroused. How he was ever going to sleep with her curled against him like this was anybody's guess! he thought, and lay very still, inhaling the sensuous perfume of her skin until her breathing grew deeper and more even.

Comforted by his warmth, exhausted by her dreams, Sanchia slid into an undisturbed sleep, waking just as it was getting light with an unfamiliar weight across her stomach.

Alex was still there, having lain beside her for hours, she realised with a small leap of excitement. But some time during the night he had rid himself of his clothes and was now lying naked under the sheet. His body was half turned towards hers, and what she could feel was the warm weight of one strong arm across her middle.

Trying not to disturb him, Sanchia moved her head to look at him, thinking how incredible he was, her eyes feasting openly on his proud, classical features: his high, intellectual forehead; that rather arrogant nose, and that sensual mouth that could condemn or thrill with a single calculated gesture.

Unable to stop herself, she stirred slightly to press her lips to the velvety texture of his shoulder, feeling the leashed power of muscle, the taut strength of his body beneath the smooth bronzed skin.

He was hard and strong and real—the only thing about her life that was, she decided wryly. She ached to touch him, and for him to touch her, wanted to wake him, yet feared the consequences to which such an action would inevitably lead.

Beneath his strong, warm arm her body pulsed with the need for greater contact. She was hot and moist, trapped in the sensual lethargy of her feverish wanting.

'Alex…' Desire overcoming fear, she whispered his name on a trembling breath, and then, driven by the deep ache within her, ran tentative fingers over the hair-roughened contours of his chest.

She was inviting trouble, she knew. But if he was trouble then she wanted all he could give her! Her hand recklessly shaped the hard line of his waist and hip, sliding across the firm, tautened muscles of his pelvis beneath the tight band of his briefs.

His briefs! So he hadn't presumed, she realised, and she liked it, her heart beating rapidly as the tight elastic yielded under her probing fingertips.

Alex emitted a deep groan from his throat the second before his hand slammed down on hers. With one effortless movement he jerked her across so that she was lying fully stretched along the length of his hard, aroused body.

'You do realise what you're doing, don't you?' he rasped, loving the way her hair cascaded down and caressed his chest.

'Yes.'

Dear God! he prayed hectically. Had she remembered?

'Why?' He wanted her to say it. To tell him that she had, and that it didn't matter.

'I want you,' she whispered, inhaling the faint spice of his angular jaw, coarsened now by a night's dark growth of stubble.

The moist eroticism of her mouth over his combined with the sensuous softness of her silk-clad body was more than a man could take, and his briefs were suddenly much too confining. He moved to dispense with them and was surprised and pleased when she had no qualms in assisting him to take them off.

Her silk nightdress rucked under his dark hand as he slid it up over the soft mound of her buttocks, his fingers caressing the smooth, responsive flesh they had exposed.

Suddenly impatient to have her naked, he tugged at the flimsy little garment and was rewarded when she lifted her arms to accommodate him, so that he could toss the impeding piece of silk aside.

Sanchia sucked in her breath as the coarse texture of his body hair grazed the sensitive peaks of her breasts.

'You're beautiful,' Alex whispered, his voice hoarse with raw need.

The soft pressure of her warm body against his aroused heat was stretching his control to the limit, and the feel of those lovely breasts moving sensuously against his chest was driving him mad.

Moving under her, he heard her sharp gasp of pleasure as his mouth closed over the swollen aureole of one heavy, engorged breast, his action sending a throbbing need through the hot, hard shaft of his manhood.

Sanchia groaned from the ecstasy, her hips grinding provocatively against his, her thighs closing around the burning evidence of his arousal as she lifted her upper body, angling her other breast for the same exquisite attention from his hot, tormenting mouth.

She was proud of her breasts, and realising how they turned him on as he suckled and kneaded their aching fullness made her feel divinely feminine, glorying in the power of her own sensuous womanhood.

'You drive me insane!' With an almost angry snarl, Alex rolled her onto her back, so that she was effectively trapped beneath him. She gave a throaty groan as sensations ricocheted through her body, uttering his name over and over until he blotted out the sound with the dominating pressure of his mouth.

Her skin felt like silk, he thought, bringing all the experience of a lifetime into play as his expert fingers moved with slow, arousing skill over the golden sheen of her body.

His lips followed the route his hands had taken, producing small sighs of wanting as they burned a path over her sensitive waist and hips, across the flat plane of her stomach to the place that dragged a deep, shocked gasp of pleasure from her, before they moved up again to claim the burgeoning softness of her perfect breasts.

How easily she responded to him, he thought with heartfelt satisfaction, his lashes dark against his cheeks as he watched the way her eyes closed in almost painful pleasure, as the pale aureoles swelled in undisguised acceptance of him as her lover.

And he *would* love her, he thought. As he should have loved her that first time. Not ravage her, as he had done then—as it would be so easy to do now, when hot and primal urges were burning him up with the need to feel himself inside her. In a way it would be a first—to make love to her without the past hanging over them like a dark spectre, and to know that she was responding to him with her mind as well as her body.

With grim determination he set out to brand her as his in a way she would never forget, guiding her through a long, leisurely dawn of sensuous pleasure until she was begging for the fulfilment she craved.

Only then, when she lay damp and sobbing for his possession, did he allow his formidable self-discipline to slide, sinking into her with a driving power that had her crying out his name, clinging to him as he took them both to the pinnacle and over the edge in a mutual crescendo of shuddering, shattering release.

CHAPTER EIGHT

'I HAVE to go over to Hamilton,' Alex told her, emerging from the *en-suite* bathroom in a fine white shirt and tie and light grey trousers that moulded his hips and thighs superbly. The jacket was hooked over one shoulder. 'It's business, but I don't want to leave you here on your own. I'd like you to come with me. You could do some shopping. Go—'

'I'll be fine,' Sanchia emphasised, still reclining in bed, smiling at his genuine concern.

'You're sure?'

Her heart swelled while her eyes feasted on the sheer physical perfection of him. Did he really care? 'Quite sure.'

He came over to her where she lay, propped up on an elbow, looking provocatively up at him with just a flimsy sheet half covering her nakedness.

'You're a temptress,' he chided softly, and tore back the sheet, allowing his eyes freedom to roam over her voluptuous curves before stooping to claim her soft mouth in a kiss that left her weak.

'And you can't get enough of me,' she asserted with shuddering pleasure because his hands were moving possessively over her again, as they had been doing since the early hours, warm and skilled and unashamedly intimate.

'Don't I just know it?' he said, with an almost grim tug of his mouth. And just how much was evident as he moved to straighten up.

'That's all right, because I can't get enough of you either,' she purred, stretching out like an alluring little cat to pull him down to her again.

His mouth on hers was hard and demanding this time, and it was with a great deal of reluctance, she realised, that he eventually dragged himself away from her.

'I have to go,' he whispered against the top of her head.

She let him do so, with a little moan of regret.

'Shall I wait for you here...*sir*?' she emphasised, with teasing in her glittering almond eyes, glad that Crystal had been given the day off to attend her niece's wedding and that there was only a part-time cleaner and the gardener on duty to witness their late appearance.

A brief smile touched his mouth, but his thick brows were drawn together in a way that made her uneasy. Was he having misgivings about what had happened? she wondered suddenly. Were her feelings for him too obvious, making him fear he might be getting in too deep?

'When I come back,' he said, scooping up a briefcase, 'you and I are going to have a serious talk.'

'What about?' she queried, frowning, remembering what he had said about taking advantage of her.

Suddenly too conscious of her nakedness, she pulled the sheet up around her. Was he going to tell her that a fling would be very nice but not to get emotionally involved with him because he didn't intend taking it any further than that?

'When I get back,' he reiterated firmly, with the hard assuredness of a man who wouldn't be swayed from his purpose once his mind was made up.

Hurry back, Sanchia wanted to say, but didn't, unsure of him, and suddenly feeling much too insecure. A few minutes later she heard the sudden burr of the speedboat as it left the jetty.

Intending to spend what was left of the morning in the pool, she had only been outside for a few minutes when an unpleasantly forceful wind drove her back in. After showering, therefore, and pulling on a loose T-shirt and shorts, she fixed herself a light lunch and then settled down in the comfortable luxury of the sitting room to sift through some photographic magazines she had already read for any articles she wanted to keep.

Hearing a car drawing up, she went over to the window. The wind was ripping through the oleanders, tearing at the long multi-coloured wrap-around skirt of the redhead who was stepping out of the taxi so that she was having a battle holding it down.

A chilling sensation crept along Sanchia's spine—some elusive memory flitting across her mind that was gone before she could grasp it.

She watched the woman climb the steps to the front porch, yet she still started when she heard the doorbell ring—the sound absurdly ominous out in the spacious hall.

'Hello, Sanchia.' The woman, who wasn't much older than herself, greeted her with what Sanchia sensed was a purely perfunctory smile.

'I'm sorry?' Studying the chic short hair and the classically striking features, Sanchia questioned the familiarity, her brows drawing together. So this woman knew her! But what was responsible for the panic she could feel rising inside her—the awful foreboding that was tying her stomach in knots?

'I know. I'm the last person you expected to see here,' the woman remarked, clearly taking Sanchia's puzzled response to mean something else. 'But I knew Alex was out at a meeting with my brother today, so I thought I'd just come over and see for myself.'

'See what for yourself?' Sanchia enquired tentatively, not sure she liked the woman's tone.

'That Danny was right.'

'Danny?' The man Alex had business with today. An ex-university colleague, Sanchia remembered him telling her.

'Yes.' Discomfort lined the striking features. 'Could you at least let me in? This infernal wind's driving me mad!'

Automatically, too taken aback to do anything else, Sanchia backed away from the door, leaving the way clear for the woman to enter. At the bottom of the steps the taxi had its engine still humming, barely audible above the gusts that were sweeping through the oleanders, tossing the petals from their pink flowers like confetti over the drive.

'He saw you and Alex in some restaurant the other night and said that Alex didn't seem too keen on Danny seeing the two of you together. At least that was what he said it looked like. He said all Alex did was utter a few abrupt words to him, grab your belongings from the table and leave, and that wasn't like Alex. Danny said he didn't look too happy.' The clear blue gaze raking over Sanchia's amply-filled T-shirt and leg-flattering shorts didn't look too happy either. 'One can only surmise why.'

'I'm not sure what you're talking about,' Sanchia uttered, her throat contracting, remembering all too clearly the way Alex had bundled her out of the restaurant that first night. She would have added, *Or who you are*, but the woman obviously thought she knew her, and some deep-buried agony forewarned her that this unwelcome visitor would somehow relish—even take advantage of—her vulnerability.

Instead she said, 'Alex isn't here,' then instantly wished she hadn't when she saw a smile that was almost derisive lift the woman's mouth and remembered she already knew about his meeting in Hamilton.

'No, sweetie, I know.' Her tone, like her smile, was uncomfortably patronising. 'I would have thought it was obvious that it's *you* I've come to see.'

'Oh?' A sudden gust caught a few fallen leaves from the drive and brought them swirling in across the tiled floor. Using all her strength to push the door closed against the wind, Sanchia folded her arms as she turned back to the woman, unfolding them again when she realised how defensive that must make her look.

'Danny said you'd been working too hard or hadn't been well or something, and that Alex has brought you here to recoup.'

'Er...yes,' Sanchia said hesitantly. After all, it was true, wasn't it?

'He's pretty magnanimous like that!'

'Yes,' Sanchia agreed again, feeling that the last remark had been made solely to demonstrate her visitor's familiarity with Alex. She wondered what was behind the searching blue eyes and that rather forced feminine laugh, because she was certain the woman wasn't here just to enquire after the state of her health.

'I hadn't realised you were even seeing each other again,' the redhead commented, flouncing into the sitting room at Sanchia's silent and reluctant invitation. 'He hadn't mentioned it to Danny or myself.'

Sanchia's slanting eyes were dark and guarded as the woman stood there in the middle of the room, studying one of the locally painted seascapes on the long wall. 'Should he have?'

'You know, I helped him choose these.' That chic head turned to look at her. 'I really thought it was over between you two.'

'Over?' Sanchia's throat worked nervously, her voice cracking over that simple word.

Was this a serious girlfriend of Alex's? she wondered, with a familiar ache starting in her temples and a queasiness in her stomach stemming from more than just what might be buried in her past. But this morning he had made love to her with earth-shaking tenderness. Even now her body still tingled from the exquisite pleasure he had shown her time after time. So why was she worrying? She loved him, and her one aim in life now, she told herself, was to make him love her in return.

'Apparently not,' she murmured, her confidence strengthened by sudden resolve.

The smile that was directed Sanchia's way was almost painful. 'You think you can keep him?' There was a hint of hysteria, Sanchia detected, surprised, beneath the woman's confident tones. Warily she watched her move over to one of the paintings, red-tipped fingers running down the edge of the frame as lovingly as if it were the hard-boned cheek of the man to whom it belonged. 'You can't really say you succeeded before, can you? So why have you suddenly turned up again after all this time?'

Beneath the thin cotton of her T-shirt Sanchia shuddered, realising she had a real opponent—even an enemy—in this beautiful and jealously possessive redhead.

Why hadn't Alex given her any inkling as to this woman's place in his life? Because she certainly seemed to have a place. And why, if he was involved with someone else, had he brought her with him to Bermuda? Made no pretence of wanting to seduce her? In fact, he had made it quite clear from the start that ultimately he intended to take her to bed!

Was this was he wanted to talk to her about? Another woman? she wondered achingly, remembering his parting words before he had left. Was that why he had been so careful about protecting her during their lovemaking, and why he had been looking less than jubilant earlier, before he'd left to go over to Hamilton? Was it guilt making him look like that? A prick of conscience over having two women on the same small island at the same time?

She remembered Hilary warning him about someone called Yasmin Croft being back here for the summer, remembered his remarks about Danny. Putting two and two together, she could only assume that this was the Yasmin to whom Hilary had referred.

'I don't see that my being here is any concern of anyone else's,' she uttered, in spite of her suddenly dwindling confidence. 'And if you have anything you want to ask Alex, then I suggest you talk to him personally.'

It was clearly not the answer Yasmin was expecting—or wanting—because suddenly she swung to face Sanchia, with a waft of heavy perfume stabbing the air.

'I think it only fair to tell you he *has* discussed marriage with me,' the woman informed her with a half-triumphant, half-tentative smile, as though she were bracing herself for a reaction but wasn't sure exactly what to expect.

'Congratulations!' Sanchia snapped back, her spirit conceal-
ing the chill spreading through her on hearing this piece of news.

'You mean you don't mind?' Surprise widened the woman's
heavily shadowed eyes.

'Why should I?' Sanchia was grateful to hear herself sounding so careless. She even managed a little shrug. 'I've got no hold
over Alex. I'm sure he'll do exactly as he pleases.'

'Because the one string you had to your bow unfortunately
snapped, didn't it?'

'Excuse me?' She didn't have a clue what the woman was
talking about. What string? What bow?

'The baby,' Yasmin stressed, her tone—her whole manner—
suddenly impatient. 'You know as well as I do that was the only
reason he married you!'

Baby? The word wasn't even audible on Sanchia's lips. The
colour draining from her face, she clutched the open door close
by as waves of nausea and dizziness threatened to overwhelm
her.

'Gosh, I'm sorry…' Through the thickening haze Yasmin Croft
sounded worried—totally out of her depth. 'I didn't realise it still
affected you like that. Look…shall I fetch you some water?'

Baby? Married?

How could it be?

Unsteadily, Sanchia tried to shake off the inertia that was
paralysing her. Her eyes were dark and enormous in the bloodless pallor of her face.

'Just go,' she managed to get out, scarcely able to take in the
other woman's discomfort as the redhead sent her a conscience-
stricken look and fled.

After she had gone, Sanchia sank down into the closest chair,
shaken and trembling, her mind racing in all directions, her
thoughts in turmoil, utterly confused.

She was his wife! She was Alex Sabre's *wife*! They'd even
had a baby! And all the time he had chosen to keep that little fact
from her! He had brought her here, not breathing a word, forced

her into loving him, and then made love to her as though it was entirely mutual—yet still he hadn't said anything—told her the truth. Why not? What reason could he have for keeping something like that from her? Unless...

Unless he was intending to reverse the situation, a little voice suggested, goading her—as soon as he could.

She thought of those nights he had gone out alone. Was it because he was seeing another woman?

If I were brutally honest you'd know it—and you wouldn't particularly thank me for it, he had said the day he'd taken her to that beach on the other side of the island.

But why would he have shown such consideration—treated her with such tenderness—if he didn't care about her? she wondered wretchedly. Why? Hadn't he told her she was his wife because he'd thought she wasn't ready for such an obvious shock? Was that why he had kept her from speaking to Danny Croft? In case the man had accidentally let it slip that they were married? Or was it simply that Alex hadn't wanted the other man to see her with him in case it jeopardised his chances with the beautiful Yasmin? Was consideration all he really felt towards her, and was it just his conscience—that daunting integrity of his—that had stopped him from divorcing her while she was still unaware even of who he was? Was that why he'd said last night that in sleeping with her he would only be taking advantage of her? Why he had looked less than comfortable this morning, when he'd said that there was something they had to talk about?

If I were brutally honest you'd know it—and you wouldn't particularly thank me for it.

A sob tore from her throat. So he had made a fool of her instead. Let her fall head over heels in love with him when he knew all the time that their days as man and wife were numbered!

The emotion that was building in her chest was almost choking her. She had to have it out with him. She didn't care who he was with or how important his meeting was. She had to confront him with it. Ask him why he had done it. Get him to tell her everything. Find out where she stood!

He answered his phone the instant she dialled his mobile number.

'Why didn't you tell me we were married?' she breathed, in a small, accusing voice.

'What?'

'Why didn't you tell me I was your *wife*?'

'Dear God.' She heard him saying something to someone else, his voice muffled as though he'd put his hand over the mouthpiece. 'You've remembered,' he said swiftly, coming back to her. 'What have you remembered?' He swore viciously under his breath. 'I knew I shouldn't have come out and left you there alone!'

'No, I haven't remembered,' she bit out, picking at the paintwork of the doorjamb beside the sitting room telephone. 'And your consideration is commendable! If you must know, Yasmin came and told me.' Bitterly she added, 'The name ring any bells?'

'Yasmin?'

'Yes. Funny, isn't it? Having to be told by your husband's mistress that you're actually his wife!'

He swore quietly again, this time quite crudely. 'Sanchia—'

'She said I had a baby! What happened to it?' she demanded on a small anguished note.

'There isn't any baby!' The statement was almost a snarl.

'Why didn't you tell me?' Her voice was trembling with tortured accusation.

'I had my reasons,' he rasped.

Yes, like wanting a divorce!

She couldn't bring herself to say that. She couldn't bear to let him know how much he meant to her and how much she was hurting.

'What reasons?' she insisted, choked.

'Look, I can't talk about this over the phone!'

No, she'd bet he couldn't.

'You lied to me!' she recriminated. The sudden deep moan

of the wind brought her injured gaze to the rear window, to the
angry grey ocean through the tossed scarlet blooms of the
Poinciana tree beyond the terrace.

'No, I didn't—'

'Yes, you did! You've made me look a fool in front of everyone! Do Chet and Hilary know?'

'Only Hilary knows we're married. Not Chet.'

'And Yasmin Croft. Have you discussed my little problem
with her?'

'No, I haven't!' He sounded extremely angry all of a sudden.

'Well, you discussed marriage with her!'

'*What?*'

'Does she know that your wife can't even remember who you
are—even without the inconvenience of not knowing that she's
married to you?'

'Of course not!'

'Really?' Only her wounded shock and anger was preventing
her from breaking down completely. 'You discussed it with Hilary.'

'That's different!'

'Is it?' she uttered, battling to contain a sob. Yet even as she
threw those bitter words at him she knew that it was. Nevertheless,
she couldn't help tagging on, 'You've made a laughing stock of
me, and I'm not sure I want to be here any longer!'

'Sanchia! Stay where you are! I'm coming back!'

'Why? So you can carry on parading your prize specimen
around for the whole island to get a good look at—laugh at!'

'You're hardly a prize specimen,' he breathed, his voice
sounding compressed, as though he were speaking with his teeth
clenched, as though he were trying to keep their conversation
from whoever was with him in the room. 'You're my wife!'

'So good of you to let me in on it!'

'Sanchia—'

'Especially now there's nothing holding us together!'

'*What?*' His swift sharp utterance sounded stretched—pecu-
liar—and a sudden pain lanced across Sanchia's temples.

Her head seemed to be buzzing with a jumble of incoherent thoughts—thoughts that were clawing at her mind like the wind she could hear clawing through the oleanders at the front of the house.

'Nothing...' Her voice was strung with pain, but whether the pain was physical or mental she couldn't tell.

'Sanchia?' Alex's tone was urgent—commanding. 'Sanchia, stay right where you are! I'm leaving now!'

'Get you!' The phone clattered back onto its rest as she cut him off just as he started to say something else.

She knew she should have obeyed, should have stayed there and waited to hear what he had to say. But the shock, hurt, anger and humiliation, coupled with the animosity she'd had to face from the woman who was apparently his mistress, was suddenly all too much to take.

She needed to get out! She *had* to! Desperation drove her out through the deserted kitchen. She needed to walk! To think!

The wind was so fierce it almost ripped the glass-paned door out of her hand, and the rain was already coming down as she left the safety of the house behind her, hitting her with stinging pellets against her bare limbs.

Words and pictures came, fragmented, into her brain, like pieces of a shredded film, regurgitated from the recycle bin of her subconscious.

Complicated. Much too complicated. They had said those things to each other the first time she had met him! And that lobster in the restaurant yesterday—he'd ordered it deliberately! Taken her there on purpose! Known how she would react—because she'd reacted in exactly the same way when he had taken her there before!

Facts came piling in, but further back. Things she had never forgotten. Growing up in so many different places because of her father's job. Coming back to London. Her parents' death: first her father, then her mother. Meeting Luke. She'd forgotten Luke. He'd been best man at a wedding where she had been the photographer, and six months later they had been planning their own wedding. Suave, handsome Luke. Honest. Hardworking. In love with her. Or so she had thought.

Her sob was lost on the howling wind, her thoughts relentless, like the driving rain, the cruel memories coming in a torrent of torturing events, like a videotape on fast forward.

Luke cheating on her; crashing the small plane he had taken up without proper authorisation somewhere over in France; killing himself five weeks before the wedding along with the nightclub singer he had been secretly seeing.

She hadn't gone to the funeral, unable to cope with the double blow. And four weeks later she'd gone on the holiday that should have been her honeymoon, alone, to this island, wanting only to escape the many questions, the unbearable condolences of friends and acquaintances back home.

It all came back too vividly. Meeting Francine and Rick, the young American couple who'd been staying in the same hotel. Being talked into attending a party she hadn't wanted to attend—hadn't even realised they had gatecrashed—only to wind up in the penthouse luxury of that South Shore hotel, having sex with a man she didn't even know.

Her memories were crushing now as that first meeting with Alex rose before her mind's eye to torment her. The pain of betrayal she had been suffering that night. The need to lash out at someone. The total abandonment of herself to a man who had swept her away in a conflagration of other needs she had never realised she possessed.

Coming back from Bermuda. Finding out she was pregnant…

The sudden memory of it slashed across her heart like the vicious blade of a knife.

Her baby! An agonised sob was torn from her, carried away by the vicious wind. How could she have forgotten her baby?

She was crying now, bitterly and uncontrollably, her legs crumbling beneath her so that she dropped down onto the wet sand, reliving it all, her ravaged face buried in her hands.

CHAPTER NINE

SHE had been working freelance for a small suburban newspaper, and had been discussing some proofs laid out on the desk in her editor's shabby little office the day Alex had turned up there looking for her.

His too well remembered voice had made her look up, startled the way he had spoken her name had been chilling and hard.

He hadn't appeared fazed, had just stood there in that superbly tailored dark suit, looking powerful and confident and incredibly charismatic, shot through with menace too, from the top of his well-groomed dark head to the tip of his black polished shoes. Because of course he had known who she was by then. He had had her traced.

All she'd been able to do was grab the back of a chair, because her knees had felt about to buckle, and breathe almost insensibly, *'You!'*

'Yes, me,' he had acknowledged deeply, without a glimmer of warmth. One glance at the editor had sent him scuttling from his own office in deference to Alex's unquestionable authority. 'So you're the woman who's responsible for most of my brother's debts. And who cared so bloody little about him she couldn't even turn up for his damned funeral!'

'Your *brother*?' It had come out in a quiver at the shock of seeing the man she had behaved so shamefully with, and whom she had thought never to see again, standing there, dominating the tiny office.

'Half-brother,' he supplied, with a smile that didn't warm the chilling depths of his stunning eyes. 'Luke Sabre. Remember him? Or have there been so many since you've lost count of their names—?' A frown brought his thick brows together as his gaze, which had been moving insolently down over her clinging sweater and jeans, came to rest on her burgeoning midriff.

'How dare you?' she seethed, hating his implication, heat stealing up her throat into her cheeks as those grey eyes continued to bore through her clothes as though he could see the changes that were taking place inside her.

'Oh, yes, I dare!' he rasped, his gaze meeting hers with a hard and frightening intensity. 'How much did he spend on you... *Sanchia*?' He hesitated over her name, emphasising it in a flaying reminder of the way she had withheld it before the blistering scene that had taken place in the intimacy of that Bermuda hotel. 'Or didn't you give a damn just so long as he could buy you all the things you wanted?'

'I don't see that that's any of your business,' she retorted angrily, letting go of the chair so that he wouldn't realise how disconcerted he was making her feel.

'Don't you?' His retort came back like whiplash. 'Then I'm afraid I have to tell you, my dear misguided girl, that it's very much my business! It was *my* money he was borrowing—in more ways than just the conventional!'

'What?' Her hand went to her throat—a hand that trembled in a gesture those shrewd eyes could hardly fail to miss. So this was Alex Sabre, she acknowledged shakily. How often Luke had mentioned him! With envy. With awe. With admiration. It probably hadn't been any coincidence that he had booked their honeymoon in Bermuda. Luke had been estranged from his half-brother, but he must have known that Alex would be there at that time, and had wanted to flaunt his new wife in front of him as one thing he had that his brother didn't. His barrister brother. Handsome. Intelligent. Tremendously wealthy. In fact, Sanchia had grown to recognize, everything that Luke had tried to emulate and had come out sorely wanting, never quite able to measure up.

'Is that little display of naïveté genuine, or just a superb piece of play-acting?' he demanded harshly. 'Didn't you even stop to question where any of that money might have come from? Or were you the one instrumental in suggesting he purloin the funds?'

'Purloin the funds?' This was becoming ridiculous! Sanchia started to feel genuinely afraid. 'I don't know what you're talking about,' she flung at him, shuddering at the way that hard grey gaze had dropped again to the incriminating width of her distended middle. 'Luke loved and respected you! He would never have taken anything from you!' *Not like he took from me,* she wanted to add, but didn't, concluding instead, 'And any money he gave me—put into our account—he earned himself!'

An account he had insisted she open with him, in joint names, she reminded herself bitterly. Because he had been working away in some high-flying job and wanted to put the significant amounts of commission he earned towards their wedding and their future, towards getting their dream home.

'I'm sorry to disillusion you, Sanchia,' the deep voice continued relentlessly, 'but Luke wasn't capable of holding a steady job. He died leaving substantial debts—mainly gambling debts—after squandering most of the inheritance that had been released to him. He borrowed from me, and when he couldn't get any more he began borrowing on investments that weren't his to borrow from. Misappropriating family funds. It didn't come to light until several weeks ago. He was weak, immature and impulsive.'

As well as a liar and a cheat, she accepted silently and then, purely by instinct, thought, *Not like you.* You'd probably sell your soul before you'd relinquish even a gram of that glaring integrity.

'Perhaps if you'd agreed to help him he wouldn't have got into so much…' *Trouble,* she'd meant to say, even then defending her ex-fiancé. But she changed it to, 'So much difficulty.'

'I did help him.' He delivered those words, with cold assurance, a bleak look in his eyes, grimness in his hard, disciplined mouth. 'Over and over. Supporting ventures that didn't come to fruition. Paying off his debts. There came a time when I knew he had to stand on his own two feet—fend for himself—and I paid for it by winding up with a brother who didn't want to know me. But for all that he was my brother, and a sucker for every woman who wanted to take advantage of his misplaced generosity.'

'But I wasn't one of them!' she shot back, refusing to stand there and listen to him bracketing her together with all the rest. 'We were going to be married. I loved him!'

His eyes glittered darkly with what she supposed was grief over losing his half-brother. But there was something else, something primitive and feral, that sent a dangerous response through her blood.

'So much that you came to bed with me?'

In the pregnant silence that followed she remembered the desperation with which she had given herself to him, and the same desperation with which he had taken her; she knew then the demons that had been driving him while she relived the feeling of his mouth on hers, the arousing warmth of his skilled hands on her body, the sensuality of his clothes against her skin.

'Luke had just died. I didn't know what I was doing,' she said, trying to vindicate herself, trying to stem the feelings that arose from reliving those shameful moments in this man's bed.

'Didn't you? Like you didn't know what you were doing when you took that extortionately priced diamond ring you were ignorant enough to let him pay for? Only it wasn't Luke who paid for it. It was me!'

She had been well aware of the cost of that ring, which had since been sold, and the proceeds sent to charity. She had tried to dissuade Luke from buying it, but he had gone ahead and done so without her knowledge. Alex, she realised, must have found the receipt when he'd been going through his brother's belongings.

'So what else did I finance?' Inexorably he went on. 'The

wedding trousseau? That nice little Mini my investigator's seen you driving around in? The trip to Bermuda you took before Luke was even cold?'

Hurting, lashed by his words then as the wind across the rain-swept beach was lashing her soaked hair across her face now, she had thrown back bitterly, 'Well, over that little matter you extracted payment in full, didn't you?' And she had earned her comeuppance when he'd suddenly reached for her, grabbing her arm before she could sidestep away from him, his jaw rigid with anger, his blazing eyes seeming to burn her with their fury.

'Is that what it was?' His teeth were clenched and his loathing seemed so thick that he could hardly speak. 'Did you know I was your fiancé's brother when you were leading me on in that bar that night?'

'I wasn't leading you on! *You* came on to *me*, if you remember! I didn't even know who you were!'

'That didn't seem to matter.'

The stinging slap she delivered across his cheek had her hand hurting for days. 'You financed a honeymoon! That was what you got! I didn't know you were Luke's brother or I wouldn't have touched you with a bargepole! And I only went to Bermuda because it had already been paid for and because I couldn't bear staying at home!'

The nausea with which she had suffered in her early pregnancy, and which had seemed for some time to have settled down, rose up in her throat, propelling her out of his grasp and into the little adjoining kitchen, where she was violently sick in the sink.

'It seems my presence always has this effect on you,' he drawled from the doorway as she rinsed out her mouth, ripped off some kitchen paper to dry her lips.

She felt too wretched to answer, flinching from the clamp of a cool hand on the nape of her neck.

'Is it Luke's?' he asked quietly, those firm, determined fingers drawing her back towards him. 'Or mine?'

It was pointless to lie, she thought, reminded that this man's

wits were honed to rooting out the truth and that he would probably be unscrupulous in his methods to achieve it.

'Luke and I hadn't seen each other for nearly two months before his accident,' she uttered weakly, conscious of the strength
in the arm that lay against her back, the unleashed power of the
male body it was taking all her control not to lean back against.
'He was working abroad. In Switzerland. Or so he said,' she
added with bitter emphasis. 'At least that's where the money he
was transferring came from. Work out the time since then, and
that would make this pregnancy at least into its sixth month! In
which case,' she went on spearing him with sarcasm even though
she was feeling so bad, 'if it were his, I'd be carrying a child of
rather stunted growth, don't you think?'

With one easy movement he pulled her round, his frown
deepening, some unfathomable emotion glinting in his eyes as
he made a pointed and disconcerting study of her figure. But then
he dipped his head in silent acknowledgement of what he had
clearly already decided. That the baby she was carrying was his.

'If you must know, your brother drained me too—of every
penny I had,' she went on, regretting having to say it, her voice
cracking from the pressure of those strong hands on her shoulders,
from the stirring excitement engendered by his fresh clean scent,
his strength, his virility. 'Check my bank statements if you don't
believe me. And I don't know why I did what I did with you. I suppose it was because I felt so wretched. Because I'd lost everything
and didn't think there was anything else to lose. Because on top
of everything else I'd found out he was seeing someone else!'

And yet those feelings for Luke had seemed to wane signif-
icantly during the weeks following her return from Bermuda.
Weeks when it had been all she could do not to dwell on the man
with whom she had committed such a mindless act and who,
though a total stranger, had awakened such passion in her, which
ever since had haunted her dreams and her conscious hours.
Even so, the thought of how his half-brother had used her still
brought stinging tears to her eyes.

She heard the hard breath Alex Sabre drew, felt the strong fingers tighten almost painfully on her slender bones.

'Wasn't that just a little bit foolish?' he put to her softly, his velvet tones cloaking a will of unbending steel.

Refusing to be intimidated, she looked him straight in the eyes, her amber gaze faltering only slightly under the unwavering strength of his as she answered pointedly, 'Yes, it was, wasn't it?'

Her meaningful response brought his head down, his lips compressing in wry acknowledgement.

'Touché,' he breathed, the deep rumble of his voice a disturbing reminder of the way he had used it to arouse her, softly, sensuously, like a trail of warm honey across her skin.

He was as much at fault and he was accepting that, she realised, fighting the fire he was igniting—heaven help her!—even in spite of his accusations.

'So you're carrying my child,' he stated grimly. 'And what exactly do you intend doing about it?'

'I'm not getting rid of it, if that's what you're implying!' she threw back, aghast. 'Don't think that just because you're rich and influential all you have to do is throw more money at me and I'll jump to do whatever you say!'

Pulling out of his grasp, she tossed the used paper into the bin, stamping on the pedal with a ferocity that sent its metal lid clanging back against the wall.

'Have I suggested anything of the sort?'

From a safer distance she viewed him challengingly, wondering exactly what he was suggesting.

'And I haven't thrown any money at you—not intentionally anyway,' he grimaced, reminding her. 'Nor was I intending to.'

'Good!' she snapped. 'Because I've no intention of asking for any—either now or in the future! So you needn't worry about that!'

'This baby needs a home,' he said simply, ignoring her outburst. 'Or are you planning on bringing it up in a rented bedsit?'

So he knew where she lived. He had done his homework, she realised with a little shudder, but was unprepared for his sudden decisive announcement, 'We'll have to start making arrangements. Even you must agree that every child needs a safe and stable home.'

'You mean…adoption?' Her eyes were wide and disbelieving. 'It's my baby. I won't—'

'No, I don't bloody well mean adoption!' His response came back like shot from a cannon. But she hadn't known then how traumatic his own childhood had been. 'We're both responsible for this child,' he reminded her tersely, 'and no offspring of mine is going to grow up adopted or under the supervision of a step-parent.'

She had been startled, she remembered, by his unbending determination as it had suddenly dawned on her what he was saying.

'You wouldn't have much choice,' she'd assured him, taken aback, 'if I decided to get married—'

'Over my dead body!'

'What?' His inexorable resolve had left her reeling and afraid.

'You're going to give it my name, Sanchia, even if you wind up hating me for it. We're going to make this child legitimate, is that clear?'

'You mean…marry you?' She couldn't believe he was suggesting—no—insisting upon it.

'That's the usually accepted way.'

'But…' Her head was beginning to swim; she couldn't think straight. Marry him? A reckless heat was trickling through every vein in her body. 'We—we don't even know each other—and I— I'm certainly not in love with you,' she protested in a wobbly voice. Infatuated, yes! And excited by him! So much so that she hadn't had a decent night's sleep for reliving the feel of his hands on her body, for remembering the hot and urgent passion that had driven them both mindless in that Bermuda hotel.

'Love has got nothing to do with it,' he answered, his tone one of cold practicality, his words only seeming to acknowledge her wild thoughts. 'And, as for not knowing each other, we can rectify that little obstacle by a couple of weeks away together—

starting next week. Think about it, Sanchia,' he recommended, before she had time to digest this startling proposal. 'What sort of a life do you think you're going to give your baby going it alone? You've no money—you just admitted that—your job takes you out all day, and I'm sure doesn't pay enough to supply you with the requisite childcare you'd need so that you could keep earning. That's if you don't find yourself facing a prison sentence. Because Luke didn't just clean you out. What he did was effectively incriminate you, Sanchia.'

Quickly her head came up, her eyes fixing on his face with painful intensity. 'You can't believe I had anything to do with that?'

He didn't answer, just stood there watching her with a cold detachment which, in spite of everything, sent traitorous tongues of desire licking through her. She didn't know whether that last statement had been a veiled threat to get her compliance, or just something he thought he'd throw in to let her know that he still hadn't made up his mind about her. She wondered what he would do if she called his bluff.

She didn't want to, though. Didn't want to risk hearing him tell her that he thought her no better than his half-brother. He was the father of her child and, scared though she was at the prospect of embarking upon a marriage that wasn't based on love, but on the consequences of one reckless hour in a stranger's bed, really, she thought, what choice did she have?

She wanted what was best for her baby, and she couldn't give it that. Alex Sabre was offering not only financial security for them both, but also his physical presence in her child's life, his home and his name. He had already admitted that love had nothing to do with it, she mused, a dull ache making itself felt around the area of her heart, but that was fine by her, because she had had enough of loving and weaving rose-coloured dreams about the future. And at least with Alex she knew where she stood. He hadn't clothed his proposal with falsehoods and sentimental claptrap, as Luke had, and she had to respect him for that.

'Well?' he pressed, his tone soft but unyielding.

She couldn't look at him as she nodded briefly in response, keeping her eyes fixed on his black shiny shoes as they moved inexorably towards her.

'Can it be so bad?' he murmured sultrily, tilting her chin with his forefinger. She met the sensuality of his smile with her heart hammering, the dark excitement of his features making her go weak. 'Who knows?' he said in honey-rich tones. 'We might even find we like each other. And we both know that in one area of our marriage we won't even have to try.'

Her eyes flashed a sudden warning at him, the depths of that dark attraction that had ensnared her before terrifying her because of her inability to resist it.

'That was then,' she uttered tremulously, her pulses racing. 'And I already explained why I behaved the way I did.'

His smile was decidedly feral. 'And you really believe that that was what it was all about?'

'Of course.' She could scarcely voice the words for the dark intensity of purpose she could see burning in his eyes.

'Then let's find out, shall we?' he invited silkily, and with one easy movement dragged her against him.

She wanted to break away. To pull herself out of the web of his spell-binding sexuality, give herself some breathing space, a few minutes to think. But as his mouth covered hers to seal their arrangement any hope she might have been harbouring to keep things on a purely practical level went up in flames.

She couldn't reason, couldn't resist, couldn't think! All she wanted, as his arms tightened around her, was to follow the instincts of her body and wallow in the dominating strength of his. To explore and rediscover that firm, insistent mouth as sensually as it was exploring and rediscovering hers.

She felt the straining of his muscles beneath the dark elegance of his jacket, knew from experience the pulsing energy and strength that was harnessed beneath the sophisticated veneer of his clothes.

He had taken her once without love—without anything but the desire to be inside her. Just as he was doing now, and the same desperate urgency for him was riding her as she massaged those tautly muscled shoulders, moaning into his mouth at the piercing sweetness that made her breasts ache for the touch of his hands and his hot mouth, at the throbbing contraction of her womb that responded too eagerly to the hard evidence of his arousal.

'Point made, I think,' he murmured softly against her lips, and she realised that he wasn't driven, or desperate to take her as he had been that first time, but very much in command of himself—almost frighteningly controlled. 'We have plenty of time for this,' he promised her, so huskily that suddenly she wondered if he was more affected than she had first thought. His words, however, awakened her to the full impact of what she had just agreed to—before the phone on the desk rang through her sudden misgivings in a harsh reminder that they were still in her editor's office.

'You'd better answer that, Sanchia,' that deep voice was suddenly advising, 'and then you can give immediate notice, or whatever it is you freelance people have to do, to terminate your contract. No arguing,' he added firmly, when he saw she was about to. 'I'm not having my wife working while she's pregnant. Besides, you've got an imminent holiday to pack for, and then a wedding to plan.'

So she had gone off to Bermuda with him, as only a few short months before she had planned to do with his brother. Except that Alex Sabre kept his promises. And while those sunny island days for Sanchia had been spent, initially, in guarded awe of him, her nights had been fevered by an increasingly abandoned and electrifying passion during the hours she'd spent in his bed.

Surprisingly, though, as the days had gone on, she had learned to relax with him. He had made her laugh, helped her to improve her swimming and shown her how to snorkel to get the best out of all the colourful marine life. And he had taken an avid interest in her bird photography. Consequently, when she'd come to the register office as his new bride, only three weeks after their return to London, it had been with the secret knowledge that she was already fathoms deep in love with him and the foolish hope that eventually she might make him love her.

Maybe it might have worked, she thought, crumpled there on the sand, if it hadn't been for the beautiful Yasmin Croft. The Bermudian-born model had been at their wedding with her brother, who'd been one of their witnesses, and had singled her out in the master bedroom of Alex's Thameside apartment, the venue for the small reception afterwards.

Offering to help Sanchia change before flying off on her three-day honeymoon in Cumbria—all that Alex had been able to spare in view of a big court case coming up—the woman had seemed amiable enough, dropping questions which at first Sanchia had thought merely conversational.

How long had she known Alex? Where were they staying exactly in the Lake District? Hadn't it been rather an exciting whirlwind romance?

The redhead's lowered gaze had run over the massive new bed that she and Alex were to be sharing in the future, and then over Sanchia's voluptuous figure, registering her swollen middle which, at five months pregnant, had been rather difficult to conceal.

'It hasn't been that long, has it?' she murmured, with an unmistakable air of patronising sweetness when Sanchia skilfully withheld exactly when and how she had met her dynamic new husband. 'But when you get to know him properly you'll realise that he's a man who puts duty first. Even if he has to make sacrifices he doesn't want to make, he'll do his duty,' the model went on to emphasise. 'It's the code by which the indomitable Alex Sabre lives. Duty to his profession, to his clients, to his own code of ethics. He'll do what's right, no matter what—even if it means jeopardising his own interests and happiness to do it. Do you understand what I'm saying?'

In the process of stuffing her make-up bag with the necessary essentials, Sanchia paused, saying hesitantly, 'No, I'm not sure I do.'

'We were engaged,' Yasmin delivered then, all amiability gone from her striking, bitterly hostile features. 'We were engaged—and he would have married me if it hadn't been for...*this*!' Her gesture towards Sanchia's midriff was denigrating and cruel. 'He isn't in love with you. He was in love with me—and he's only marrying you because you're pregnant!'

That last shocking truth, as the model slammed out of the room, was one Sanchia knew she had to cope with. After all, hadn't she known why Alex was marrying her from the very beginning? But what she hadn't reckoned on—wasn't able to deal with—was his being in love with someone else.

When she challenged him about it as he reached for her in the four-poster bed of the Lakeland hotel where they spent their wedding night, he brushed it aside as unimportant, wanting to dismiss it while she couldn't let the subject drop.

'For heaven's sake, Sanchia! What is it you want me to say?' he flung at her eventually. 'That we've been lovers? Will that satisfy you? I'm married to *you*, aren't I? And I wasn't aware that our arrangement included sharing confidences about past relationships.'

'If they *are* past,' she emphasised accusingly.

'Meaning?' His tone left no room for evasion.

'Meaning *were* you engaged to her when you met me and *are* you still in love with her?'

His voice was almost menacingly soft as he demanded, 'What kind of question is that?'

'A simple enough one, I would have thought!' she shot back at him, unaware of how her low-cut nightdress with its coffee lace edging exposed the angry rising of breasts made even more than usually voluptuous by her advancing pregnancy.

'Why?' That sensual mouth turned suddenly mocking. 'Would you be jealous if you thought another woman could still hold my interest?'

'Of course not!'

Those grey irises darkened to charcoal. 'Then why the sudden interrogation?' Propped up on an elbow, he turned towards her, gloriously naked down to where the covers lay across him, just below his navel. 'Unless it's just a smokescreen to hide the fact that my beautiful wife has suddenly had second thoughts?'

No, only that she's in love with you! her heart had clamoured, so she had to turn aside, battling to keep him from guessing at the tumultuous emotions that were stamped too clearly on her face.

'There isn't anything to have second thoughts about,' she murmured, her tone resigned. 'We both married out of duty.' How easy it was to throw those same words back at him that had been used so cruelly by his mistress!

'Duty? Is that how you see it?'

'Of course. Why else would I have married you,' she said, keeping her tone flat, 'if it wasn't for the baby.' And, with her head still averted to hide the pain that was ravaging her smooth-skinned features, 'You're not the only one round here who had plans for a different life!'

Cruelly he caught her chin between his thumb and forefinger, forcing her back to face his remorseless scrutiny.

'I see.' There seemed to be some clarification in that simple statement, but of what, Sanchia wasn't sure. 'And supposing I asked my wife on her wedding night if she's still in love with another man?'

'What?' she whispered incredulously, because that was the last thing she had imagined him asking her.

'You heard me.' Was that a veiled threat beneath those deceptively soft tones? 'Are you?'

'Am I what?' Her voice seemed to tremble from the intensity of his cold analysis.

'Are you still harbouring misplaced feelings towards my undeserving brother?'

'Don't be ridiculous,' she breathed, almost inaudibly. How

could he imagine that? After the way Luke had treated her? 'Would I be here with you if I were?'

His soft laugh was derisive. 'I don't think we'd better get into that one, Sanchia.'

Of course. That first time in Bermuda. But what she couldn't tell him right then was that what she had felt for his half-brother had never really been love; she had never known the meaning of real wanting—never come wholly alive—until she had met him that night.

'That was different,' she said, realising how effectively he had turned the tables on her. And why had he done it, she asked herself, if not to gloss over the uncomfortable subject of his own feelings for another woman? 'It's different now.'

'How?' he asked harshly. 'How is it different?'

'Because Luke…Luke isn't…here any more,' she got out awkwardly. Couldn't he see that even if she did still have some feelings for his half-brother—which she didn't—it wasn't like marrying someone while the person you really wanted was still waiting in the wings!

'Then do something for me, Sanchia. Look me in the eyes and tell me you're not still in love with my brother.'

And risk letting him see how much she wanted him—her husband—having found out in the cruellest way, by his very evasion, that his feelings for Yasmin Croft were still very much alive?

'No.' She refused. Because if he realised the truth she would never be able to bear the humiliation of his knowing she loved him in spite of his feelings for the lovely model.

'Luke's dead,' he stressed curtly, misunderstanding as she had meant him to. 'I think that's the word you were looking for, Sanchia—*dead*—while you and I are very much alive! So if you want to nurse some misplaced loyalty to a man who wouldn't have cared less if he'd got you slung in jail then go ahead. But not in our bed—and certainly not on our wedding night! And if you think that's harsh, or that I'm going to let any past lover on either of our parts undermine the one aspect of our relationship we might have working for us, then think again, darling. You know as well as I do that I just have to touch you to make your body sing its allegiance to me. And if you're still in any doubt about that, then I'll prove it to you—right now!'

And he had, she remembered achingly, shuddering from the violence of her emotions as she recalled how purposefully he had set out to extract every ounce of submission from her—and had succeeded in his purpose. Not just that first night, when he had seemed almost to mock her in his victory, but through the subsequent days of the bittersweet honeymoon that had followed.

He had taken her without words, using both passion and exquisite tenderness to arouse her, even though she'd known that it was only his ego he was salving in proving what he could do to her, and she had grown reticent and increasingly humiliated at the knowledge that he could use her so intimately when she knew he would rather have been with someone else.

The day they had flown back from Cumbria she had finally moved all her things into his apartment, and unexpectedly, as they'd been going to bed, he had removed his belongings from the master suite and said in response to her shocked and silently questioning expression, 'I believe I've given you a very pleasurable honeymoon, Sanchia, so I think I've done my *duty*.' Cruelly he had reminded her of the word she had used on their wedding night. 'The very next time we make love, dearest,' he had thrown over his shoulder before he strode out and left her, lost and alone in the enormous bed, 'you're going to come to *me*!'

But she hadn't, she reflected, the memories still torturing her. Not until this morning. Not until—with no memory of the past or even of who he was—she had grown to trust him, fallen in love with him again. Not that she had ever stopped loving him, she agonized. Because right from that very first morning, when she had walked into that courtroom and he had challenged her for being there, some intrinsic part of her had acknowledged him even though her mind hadn't. She had *known* him—with every-thing in her that had ever been his.

But the past had reared its ugly head again, with all its ugly implications. And how he must be gloating now! she realised, tor-mented, after the way she had seduced him so eagerly this morn-ing, initiating their uninhibited lovemaking and effecting her own surrender—which was what he had wanted from her all along!

The rain stung her with cruel fingers and the wind was slic-ing, but it was nothing compared to the tempest that was raging inside her as more memories collided with others that were no less bitter and harsh.

The endless nights in that empty bed. The depravity of want-ing him while she lay there alone with his child growing inside her—because surely the only reason he had abandoned her now that they were back in England was so that he could take up his affair with the model where he had left off. After all, whatever happened from then on, he had made his child legitimate. So what did it matter how he treated the child's mother? For all she knew he was still harbouring doubts about the part she might have played in his brother's deceit, no matter how much she might have thought she had convinced him otherwise. But his son or daughter would have his name—grow up under his su-pervision—and that was all that mattered.

That Yasmin had still been on the scene Sanchia had been cer-tain; she'd wondered when she heard Alex come in, sometimes in the early hours, if he had taken solace in the other woman's arms after a hard day in court. But her pride hadn't let her chal-lenge him about it further, and she had used the excuse of mar-rying him on the rebound when he taunted her about her refusal to invite him back into her bed, using her long-diminished feel-ings for Luke as a shield against the devastating emotions and needs that racked her for his older brother.

Sometimes she'd wondered whether if she had swallowed her pride and gone to him, as he had been silently demanding—let him know that the feelings she'd had for Luke were insignificant compared with the way she felt about him—she might have been able to make their marriage work. But if she had been foolish enough to hope that when her baby was born there might be a chance for them to have a real marriage, then those hopes had been wrenched from her—cruelly and heartlessly—when she had lost the baby.

She could still remember the pain, relived it all in an agony of memories. The turmoil that had been her marriage. And the wrenching pain that tore at her now was just the pain of her breaking heart.

Perhaps they might have had a chance, she thought, if her baby had survived. But disillusionment and despair had only brought about a deepening of resentment, evoking rows that were bitter and unresolvable, each blaming the other for what had happened, which had only widened the monumental gulf between them. With her baby—the only string to her bow, as Yasmin had so unkindly put it—no longer an issue, the husband she'd loved and yet had barely got to know had become no more than a stranger to her. A hard, ruthless stranger she'd seen only at breakfast, if she was lucky, who flayed her with his cold politeness and who made no more suggestions—either taunting or otherwise—about sharing his bed.

Eventually, only a couple of months after her marriage, unable to bear the situation, she had fled to Scotland, thinking herself far enough away until his agents had traced her there.

She remembered how she had felt when he had turned up at the guest house where she had been staying, the confrontation that had ensued at his reminder that she was his wife, and his demand that until things were sorted out she should return with him. She had told him she would think about it, arranging to see him the next day because that was the only condition under which he had agreed to leave. But seeing him again had opened up torturous wounds—the pain of losing her baby, of her foolish hopes and her agonising love for him—and she had known that if she kept to their agreement she would have no defence against his hard persuasion, that it would be like allowing him to lead her to her own slaughter.

And so she had packed up her few belongings and left before he was due to call, not knowing how merciful one careless step off a pavement a few days later could be. Not until now, as the memories came back to haunt her, and left her sobbing out her futile grief for only the storm to hear.

CHAPTER TEN

AS THE boat thundered through the storm, Alex didn't care that
the rain and the fierceness of the spray were soaking him. He
was gritting his teeth in defiance, letting the elements do their
worst.

He'd blown it! he thought, berating himself for his stupidity
in thinking he could get away with not telling her, in believing
he could get her to trust and respect him first. He should have
known better!

It took all his skill to manoeuvre the boat around the jetty in
the buffeting wind, and he steeled himself for the questions he
knew must come.

He should have told her, he reproached himself again. As soon
as he'd realised her amnesia was real and not affected. Shelved
his own selfish motives and chanced whatever risk there was in
telling her the truth there and then.

The wind tore through his hair and his sodden shirt as he teth-
ered the boat, with anger and regret harshening his practised
movements. Dear God! Had he been so wrong in wanting her to
look at him with the same limpid eyes with which he had sometimes caught her looking at him in those days preceding their
wedding? In wanting to feel her body grow taut with desire for
him again—if only for a while?

The house felt deserted as he entered it from the garden,

not even pausing to close the door. Even before he went through each room, calling out her name, he knew the place was empty. He could always feel her presence, and the house was devoid of it, of her warm sensuality that heated his blood and fuelled his body's throbbing impulses whenever she was around.

'Sanchia!'

Her purse and mobile phone were on the bedside cabinet, the bed still rumpled, he noted with an involuntary stirring in his loins as he thought about their abandoned loving that morning. So she hadn't taken a taxi anywhere. Which must mean she was still around here somewhere. Somewhere out there in the storm! he realised fearfully, his swift deduction sending him back down the stairs two at a time.

He couldn't forget the last thing Sanchia had said to him over the phone about nothing holding them together—or the way she had said it. Was it just something that interfering redhead had told her? Or had the confrontation somehow resurrected her memory? Brought back everything that her subconscious—that *he*—had until now protected her from?

The garden door was standing half open, and he beat it wide with his fist, shattering one of the glass panes as desperation drove him outside.

Damn that woman to hell! He should have been here! he remonstrated, mentally flaying himself. If anything happened to Sanchia... It was agony just to think about, when he knew he'd only have himself to blame.

The sea, usually so blue, was surging in a grey mist as he plunged through the storm-ravaged garden, while the wind came like voices in pain, whipping through the bright bushes of hibiscus and bending the poinciana tree beside the terrace with no regard for their fragile blooms.

He kicked off his shoes and left them where they lay in the scrub that gave onto the beach, along which he tore now as if unseen demons were after him, yelling out her name.

The wind seemed to mock him as it carried the deep sounds away from him—sounds that fell on deaf ears, because the long curve of sand was deserted and he was beginning to despair.

He thought of the lengths she had gone to before to keep him out of her life, about the pitiful thing their marriage had been, and wondered what her reaction would be if she had remembered it. She had been bitterly unhappy because he had never succeeded in filling the void that Luke had left in her heart, or in securing the trust that had been so badly shattered by his brother. She had chosen to believe the jealous ravings of Yasmin Croft and had been all too ready to tar him—and probably all men, he suspected—with the same brush because of the way Luke had behaved. Anger and resentment burned through him towards his half-brother for the way he had treated her, for the feelings Sanchia had obviously shown him that he—her husband—had never been shown. But would finding herself back in the situation she had taken every measure to escape from drive her to do anything drastic?

Rivulets coursed over the hard bones of his cheek as he sent a sudden horrified glance seawards. She was a good swimmer, but she wouldn't have gone into the water in this storm, surely? Not unless she wanted to…

His thoughts stopped him dead. Swinging towards the shore-line, he pulled himself up suddenly, catching sight of something further along the beach.

Almost obscured by the white torches of some flowering yuccas, she was lying face down, draped over a rock, her head resting on her bent arm.

'Sanchia.' He could only whisper her name now, instantaneous relief giving way to fear. But as he propelled himself forward, his powerful legs closing the distance between them, he noticed that her body was shaking with convulsive sobs.

She was soaked through, and he swore violently and without a second's delay stooped to pick her up.

He was worried by how limp she felt, and was therefore relieved to realise that she at least had some life left in her when she started to resist with weak, ineffectual thumps at his shoulder.

'Put me down. I hate you!'

So she had remembered. 'I know.'

His acknowledgement sounded cold and remorseless, and, already chilled from her memories more than her wet clothes, Sanchia shivered violently.

'I lost my baby.' They were desolate words against the rock-hard strength of his shoulder.

'Our baby,' he corrected gently, striding effortlessly with her back across the sand.

'You didn't carry her for all those months,' she sobbed, her loss excruciating. 'You didn't love her as much as I did!'

'Didn't I?' His words were rasped, the powerful muscles of his chest and arms hardening from the emotion he was reining in. 'You think you have the monopoly on feelings, Sanchia? That only you were born with the capacity to love and hate? And, while we're on the subject of hate, my darling, you only hate me because I made you feel alive when you wanted to wallow in what Luke—what you wanted to believe *I*—had done to you!'

'That's not true!' She struggled against the restraining arms that were hard and determined under her bare legs. Somewhere, she realised, she had lost her mules. 'Put me down!'

'And leave you to the mercy of the elements? You could die out here.'

'Then let me go! I want to!'

'And I'd want to turn you over my knee if I thought for one moment you were serious in that self-pitying little statement.' Relentlessly those strong legs kept covering the sand.

'You're nothing but an arrogant bully! You always were!'

'That's better.' His voice held a trace of irony. 'I don't think I need ask whether you've got your memory back, need I, Sanchia? Which means that you and I are going to have that talk. But first we're going to get you out of these clothes and into a hot bath.'

'We?' An emotion as hot as the bath to which he had referred heated her chilled body, breaking through the numbness inside. But she didn't like how his freshly acknowledged marital status seemed to give him licence to act as though he owned her, and pointedly she tagged on, 'I can manage on my own!'

'Maybe, but you might want to drown yourself.'

'And give you the satisfaction?'

She saw his mouth turn grim, felt his chest expand as though he was battling with some very strong emotion, before he murmured in a voice soft with meaning, 'There's only one satisfaction you'll be giving me.'

'No!' As they came up through the dripping garden Sanchia squirmed in his grasp. How could he imagine that she would just fall back into his bed now that she had remembered everything about their life together?

'You weren't objecting this morning.'

'That was different.'

'Why?'

'Because I didn't know you were the man I ran away from!'

He made a cynical sound down his nostrils. 'No, you knew me for who I was. And you still wanted me.'

'You made sure I would!'

'What are you saying?' Water from his hair dripped down her neck as he bore her—resisting—across the drenched terrace. 'That the whole time we've been here it's all been a calculated act on my part just to get you into bed?'

She didn't know what to think. She only knew that nothing would have changed. That, even turned on as he was by his wife, he still intended to divorce her. After all, he'd already discussed marriage with his long-standing mistress, hadn't he? Wasn't that evidence enough?

'Keep still!' he commanded roughly, when she wriggled more forcefully against his strong hold. 'There's broken glass here.'

She looked down at the lethal shards as he brought her across the threshold, saw that he was barefoot, as she was, and immediately stopped resisting, letting him pick the safest path inside.

'Was it the wind?' she asked, frowning, as he set her down on the kitchen tiles, out of harm's way.

'A particularly violent blast,' he responded with a grimace, not wishing to admit how demented he had felt when he'd realised his actions—or lack of them!—had driven her out there in the storm. 'Don't ever do that to me again, Sanchia,' he warned softly, unable to help himself in spite of it. 'Don't ever give me a scare like that again or I'll—'

'Or you'll what?' Her chin lifted above her slender neck, those slanting eyes viewing him in wounded challenge.

He didn't answer, but his grey eyes turned as dark as the clouds that were still sweeping in with the driving rain over the sea.

With his hair plastered to his scalp and his drenched shirt and trousers emphasising the contours of his powerful body, he looked, Sanchia thought, like a marauding buccaneer, bent on rape and plunder, rather than a prominent barrister from the sophisticated world he usually inhabited. Although he could do his fair share of plundering there, too, she remembered grudgingly.

Involuntarily, her eyes slid along his hard, lean length, noting with a cruel and piercing pleasure the crisp hair of his chest above the half-fastened shirt that her hands had so eagerly explored that morning. She could still remember how his body had tasted beneath her tongue. Remember the power of those hips and their grinding strength as he took her with driving possession—not just this morning, but every night of that first holiday together here, and during that bittersweet honeymoon when, stunned, and with every impulse fighting him because of what Yasmin Croft had told her, they had still made love with a fever that had ridiculed the lack of any emotion. On his part, at any rate, she thought achingly, noticing then the red streaks across the expensive fabric of his trousers.

'You—you've cut yourself.' Amber eyes lifted anxiously to his, searched and saw the blood that flowed freely from the cut on his hand. 'You're bleeding.'

'It's nothing.'

'Nothing?' She caught his long dark hand in hers, turning it to inspect the wound he had sustained just above his strong knuckles. 'How did you do this?'

'Sanchia, go upstairs.'

'Not until I've seen to this. It's terrible!' She had a strong suspicion it was something to do with her, and her forehead puckered as she looked anxiously up at him. 'Doesn't it hurt?'

'I'll live,' he assured her dryly, not trusting himself to say anything else.

He didn't want her tender ministrations. It was all he could do not to carry her upstairs himself, peel off her wet clothes and force her into accepting that she belonged to him—with him—after the way she had driven him crazy with worry out there. Having her touch him was straining every last ounce of his self-control.

Her hair and clothes were soaked and her T-shirt was clinging to her, revealing the outline of her beautiful breasts. It didn't help that their hardened tips were thrusting against the wet fabric, whether because she was cold or because she was actually turned on from that thorough examination she'd given him just now, he couldn't tell. But the thought of how responsive she was—how responsive she had always been with him—and the knowledge that he would only have to take her upstairs again to have her sobbing that response for him and only him was driving him mad.

'I said it's all right.' His voice was thick and husky. 'Now, go and get out of those clothes before I rip them off you myself!'

She didn't stay to see if he would carry out the threat.

She was soaking in the deep, marble-enclosed bath in the *en-suite* bathroom, her eyes closed, her brain churning over the things that for so long had lain buried in her subconscious, when she heard Alex come in and close the door quietly behind him.

Disconcerted by the implied intimacy, she darted a swift glance over her shoulder to where he stood, tall and powerful, leaning back against the door. Like a jailer, she thought. Blocking her escape.

He had changed out of his wet clothes, and her stomach did a crazy somersault when she saw that he had substituted them for a loose fitting black shirt and black trousers that unfairly heightened his already flagrant sexuality.

Sanchia turned away, her voice shaking a little as she said, 'When were you going to tell me?'

There was a moment's hesitation, when his breath seemed to quiver through his lungs. 'When you'd got to know me sufficiently enough to trust me.'

'Trust you?' Her swept-up hair moved softly as she turned to look at him with wide, accusing eyes. 'When you'd been lying to me?'

'I've never lied to you.' His tone was soft, yet unequivocal. 'Only by omission, when I felt it might be unwise for your health if I were to hit you with information you might not have been ready for.'

'You said we barely knew each other.'

'Because we didn't. We didn't really know each other at all. Our marriage started to flounder when our vows had scarcely finished being uttered.'

Which was true, she thought wretchedly, watching the water from the sponge she was holding trickle back into the bath with hurt and unseeing eyes. He hadn't lied about that.

'You didn't even tell me we'd been to bed together—let alone about…the baby.' She seemed to be drowning in a well of pain, of freshly resurrected and delayed grief.

'It wasn't what you wanted to hear,' he assured her softly. 'When you first asked me about our relationship, that day at court, I wasn't even sure that you weren't just pretending not to know who I was. You looked at me with such revulsion that I couldn't believe how desperately you wanted to deny all knowledge of me—whether consciously or otherwise. I thought I'd play along with your game for a while—that was until I came to terms with the fact that you really didn't know who I was.'

'And when was that?' she asked in a small, brittle voice.

'When you realised how easily you could get me to fall back into your arms because I couldn't remember how miserable I was being married to you?'

She heard him move away from the door, didn't look at him as he came and took up a position on the white brocade boudoir chair between the towel rail and the window next to the bath, so that she couldn't fail to see him out of the corner of her eye.

'It didn't surprise me that you responded to me, Sanchia. You always did. Even when you were spitting venom at me for things there was no foundation for.' She shut her eyes tightly, took a breath. *No foundation for!* 'You couldn't help yourself,' he said. 'Just as I couldn't. But, no, it was before that. I think I knew from the very beginning—or at least I knew that something wasn't quite right. You would never have come into court to sit on a jury without checking first whether or not I was defending—unless you hated me so much you wanted to put me off my stride.'

Her eyes were veiled by long lashes as she chanced a wounded glance in his direction. He was sitting with an arm supported by the back of the chair, one long bent leg resting casually over the other. His masculinity was somehow intensified by the femininity of that piece of furniture.

'Did you really think me capable,' she murmured sadly, 'of doing something like that?'

Those darkly intent eyes captured hers, and there was such suppressed emotion in their depths that Sanchia felt her throat contract. His hair was still damp, curling darkly against the nape of his neck, she noticed, swallowing, and felt the tingling in her breasts beneath the soapy water and the throb of tension in her lower body when he still didn't answer, though that clear gaze continued to hold hers.

Outside, the wind's strength was decreasing. The branches of the trees moved less violently beyond the frosted glass, while somewhere among the bright heads of the poinciana a kiskadee was shrieking, its repetitious notes emphasising the sensuality of the silence that stretched interminably between her and Alex.

'Where did you go?' he asked quietly at length. 'When you disappeared that day?'

Closing her eyes again, Sanchia turned away. She didn't want to have to remember. But there was no shield of amnesia to hide behind now, and after all he was her husband. He had a right to know.

'I went up to the Hebrides,' she told him painfully.

And how desperately she had welcomed the harsh remoteness of those islands, wanting to escape the harsher remoteness of a man whose reason for marrying her no longer existed. But she had been afraid that he would come after her. He had, after all, managed to trace her on two occasions before. It had been from there, a few days later, therefore, that she had sent a letter to him through her London solicitor, advising him not to try to find her, that she wouldn't oppose a divorce.

'I stayed...' One smooth, tanned shoulder lifted in a shrug. 'I don't know...a few days, maybe? Then I paid someone who was crossing to Ireland in a fishing boat to take me with them.'

And it had been there, a couple of days later, that she had woken up in that Belfast hospital, with all the agony of her immediate past mercifully erased.

'The driver of the car said I just stepped off the pavement without looking,' she went on, unable to tell Alex that it was because she had been crying as she'd tried to cross that road—crying bitterly—over him. She had been thinking of him receiving that letter, wishing she could retrieve it. The finality it had signified, on top of losing her baby, an agony that had been too much to bear. 'I knew there was something I'd been running away from, but I had this terror inside me that I couldn't explain and it stopped me from trying to find out.'

'And there was nothing linking you to me?'

A few dark strands of hair cascaded onto her shoulder with the barest movement of her head.

'All my papers—everything—were still in my maiden name,' she admitted with a grimace, because during those brief traumatic weeks of her marriage she hadn't bothered to have them amended. Even her passport, which she had obviously renewed between leaving Alex and having that accident, was still in her maiden name.

'And so now you've remembered.' The chair protested as he uncoiled his large frame, but she kept her eyes trained on the frosted glass of the window. 'Everything?'

His question brought her head sharply round. 'What do you mean?'

'How good we were together?' He was vacating the chair, the impact of his striking presence heightened by the casual tailored elegance of his clothes. 'What you had with me in spite of your unwillingness ever to admit it?'

He was moving over to her and she glanced away, a warning heat creeping over her skin as she said dismissively, 'That was just sex.'

'Was it?' he asked roughly, moving closer. 'Was it just sex this morning?'

For you it was, obviously! she thought achingly, thinking what a fool she had been to imagine it could be anything more than that.

'What do you want from me?' She sent an angry glance up over his hard body that was far too close for comfort, stopping just short of his disturbing eyes. 'An admission of undying devotion as well?'

'As well as what?' he rasped, unaware of what it had cost her emotionally to say it. 'Your total rejection of my devious sexual advances this morning?'

He wasn't going to let her forget how she had instigated what had happened, she realised, humiliated. Oh, why hadn't she remembered before she had offered herself to him so readily? Why, oh, why had she had that dream? And she knew now what it was she had been searching for in that endless corridor of her nightmare, recognised the significance of that agonised feeling of loss. It was the loss of both the man she loved and her baby.

'Pass me that towel.' Emotion thickened her words, and her features were ravaged by it as she pushed herself up out of the water, keeping her head high so that he wouldn't guess how disconcerted she was about his seeing her glistening nakedness.

From the way one masculine eyebrow arched, he clearly didn't think too much of the manner in which she had asked, but it was the way his eyes ran over her before he turned away that made her breasts tighten and peak shamefully in response.

As he snatched the towel from the rail, her attention was brought sharply to the angry red line across the back of his hand.

So he had managed to stem the bleeding, she thought, stepping out of the bath, silently sympathising with how sore the wound must be. But as she reached to take the towel he held out to her all sympathy for him fled when he suddenly withdrew it.

'Give me that!'

'No.' There was a kind of warped satisfaction in the way his passionate mouth firmed. 'What I want,' he breathed, moving so fast that she scarcely had time to register his actions as he whipped the towel around her and used it to draw her towards him, 'is honesty.'

Her hands flew up to push him away, but they were being crushed against his chest, and her protest was lost beneath her screaming need for him as his mouth came down determinedly over hers.

Sensations fired to life inside her as his kiss deepened and demanded, bringing her arms up around his neck, her body straining against the long, hard length of his in reckless abandonment.

He groaned deep into her throat, hard fingers tugging at her hair until the heavy curtain collapsed under their ruthless plunder and fell about her shoulders. Drawing her closer, his arms tightened inexorably across her back.

There was something shatteringly sensual in her wet nakedness saturating the immaculate tailoring of his clothes, even before he caught her slippery buttocks and pulled her into the thrusting pressure of his arousal.

She gave a small guttural sob, every sense heightening, every pulse throbbing in feverish anticipation of her fate.

'*This* is honesty, Sanchia.' His mouth was against the scented dampness of her shoulder, his skilled hands and deep voice arousing her so that she arched her back, whimpering her need for more of his galvanising caresses. 'At least your body's honest.' It was a formidable reminder of her hopeless inability to resist him, and then his mouth swooped to claim what was so willingly being offered.

Honesty, he had said, and her body demanded that from her, even if her brain staunchly refused to accept it. Because if it didn't, and she told him the truth—told him how much she loved him—then she would have nothing left. No pride. No dignity. Nothing.

'You want me,' he ground out against the smooth alabaster of her breast, his breathing laboured, his face flushed as he lifted his head, his fingers in her hair dragging her head up, forcing her to meet the naked need in his eyes that mirrored the depth of her own. 'You want me, and I'm going to prove it to you beyond all reasonable doubt!'

She made a token gesture of protest as he lifted her off her feet, but it was only a token.

Because how would he believe it? she thought hopelessly. When she was writhing beneath him again on the big bed in his room, breast straining against his suckling mouth, legs fanning open in response to those probing fingers that recognised all too easily her readiness for his possession.

She would always be a slave to her desire for him because— as he knew only too well—she couldn't help herself. The only redeeming factor was that he didn't know just how much she loved him! she agonised, and shock waves of pleasure filled her body as he broke through the last vestige of her mental denial and pushed into her.

After that it was nothing but an interrogation of the senses, one she fought to resist, with his ruthless will challenging hers for the proof he was determined to wrest from her. But her love for him empowered him, giving him sway over her heart, her mind and her body, until she felt the pressure building inside her, felt the white-hot inferno of desire tingle along her thighs. She heard herself cry out as one deep, hard thrust pushed her over the edge, wrenching the truth from her in the most elemental way until she collapsed, stripped and sobbing and gasping with him, from their protracted, earth-shattering orgasm.

CHAPTER ELEVEN

THE Crofts' party was as glamorous an affair as Alex always remembered them being. He had turned down several lunch and dinner invitations since coming back to Bermuda, but he was damned if he was going to turn down this party tonight.

Now there was no reason to. He intended to show the world—and everyone who cared to sit up and take notice—that Sanchia was back where she belonged, at his side, that she was still his wife, still legally his.

In the car beside him, Sanchia bit her lip, wishing she hadn't let Alex bulldoze her into accompanying him as he brought the car off the road flanked by sprawling mansions onto a drive between pristine lawns and tall waving palms. She didn't want to be anywhere that included Yasmin Croft.

The house was equally as grand as its neighbours, yet without the seclusion of Alex's quiet luxurious hideaway. A house, Sanchia decided waspishly, like the eye-catching clothes and jewellery of the two glittering redheads who met them at the door, designed for show.

'We're so glad you could come,' Yasmin breathed, with none of the sincerity of the elegantly maternal figure at her side. Her smile was over-bright, her expertly shadowed eyes filled with wounded suspicion as they darted from the sheer physical impact of Alex, in a white dinner jacket, bow-tie and black trousers, to Sanchia in a figure-hugging yet simple black dress, and back again to the tall man at her side.

Her injured gaze resting on the only guest she clearly wanted to entertain, she said, in more subdued tones, 'It's good to see you, Alex.' She looked and sounded, Sanchia thought, like a child who had been caught doing something she shouldn't and had been severely reprimanded for it, and something told her Alex had come down hard on the lovely model for calling uninvited at the house.

She was glad when Danny came to their rescue, his hand outstretched to greet her. 'Sanchia.'

She took his hand as they were drawn into the house, returning his genuinely warm smile as he stooped to lightly kiss her cheek.

'Alex said you hadn't been well, but I'd say you're looking positively blooming!'

He was Alex's friend, and she remembered—apart from the wedding—meeting him several times during their marriage. With brown hair and warm brown eyes, he had inherited both his good looks and his character, Sanchia suspected, from the older man who was pouring drinks outside the marquee she could see through open doors leading onto a very large and formal garden.

'It's good to see you again,' Danny added with marked sincerity. 'I didn't actually intend to ignore you that first night you got here, but I didn't see you until it was too late, and then Alex seemed very bent on whisking you away.'

Alex's smile was fleeting and he tucked her arm back into his, those stunning grey eyes holding hers—deliberately, she felt— as he responded, 'We wanted to be alone.'

And why not? Danny's smile seemed to say as he looked from one to the other of them. They had been separated, after all. But although the look Alex gave him challenged any sort of response, Danny Croft, Sanchia guessed, wouldn't be so imprudent as to mention it.

The raw longing on his sister's face, however, was only too apparent, and seemed merely to intensify as the evening progressed. Whenever Sanchia glanced her way the model's eyes were resting almost painfully on Alex, who seemed not to notice. Or, if he did, then he was certainly avoiding looking at her.

Was he making her suffer? Sanchia wondered at one point, sipping champagne in the sensuously lit garden where people were dancing to a live duo under the stars. Was he making her pay for calling on his wife when he had probably instructed her not to? She might almost have felt sorry for the woman had it not been for the fact that the redhead's intention from the first had been to make *her* suffer.

'Yasmin looks quite cut up,' she commented shakily as Alex, having insisted she dance with him, brooked no opposition and pulled her into his arms. 'Was that your objective?'

He made a cynical sound down his nostrils as he turned her on the sprawling patio. 'I'm not responsible for her well-being.'

She glanced across at the model, who was standing, her lovely face wrought, unable to take her eyes off the two of them, just outside the marquee.

Her breath catching painfully as she turned back and met the cruel beauty of those coldly remorseless features, Sanchia murmured, 'Oh, but I think you are.'

His mouth moved without humour, his dark jaw uncompromising above the stark whiteness of his shirt collar. 'Why do you think I brought you here, Sanchia?' he asked flatly, and she wasn't sure whether he was talking about the party or Bermuda in general.

'To try and bring my memory back so that you wouldn't feel such a heel divorcing me?' she supplied with mock sweetness, though she was hurting as much as the woman he was doing such a good job of ignoring. 'To let the people who matter see us together, so that when we do go our separate ways you won't have to suffer the stigma and humiliation of a deserting wife!'

He laughed very softly, as though she amused him. 'There's only one person here that matters.'

'Really? And who's that?' She smiled a challenging little smile and looked in the direction of the marquee, her eyelids heavy from the crucifying pain she felt inside. 'No, let me guess.' Yasmin was still watching them, sipping a Martini beside a young man in whom her lack of interest was blatantly obvious.

'Since you already seem to know, why ask?'

'I know that the only reason you married me was because I was pregnant.'

'Naturally.' His tone was deep, the word carelessly drawled. 'What other reason could there have been?'

Pain lanced through Sanchia, almost robbing the breath from her lungs. 'So now it doesn't matter any more, does it?'

'It would seem not.'

How easily he could say it! Hurting, she retorted bitterly, 'Why don't you go to her, then?'

She could feel cold, tense anger bubbling through the tailored cloth spanning his powerful shoulders. 'I don't know! She'd be warm, and very generous with her favours.' His anger was all too evident now. 'But I'm a thoroughly monogamous guy—and you're right! I *do* intend for everyone to see us together. Because right at this moment I'm married to *you*, and I'll be damned if I'll let you sully our marriage with snide comments like that, or screw up everything I've done to make you—and them—aware of who I want to be with. And right now that's my wife! Is that understood?'

She couldn't answer, too struck by the strength of his possessiveness, his desire to state to the world what was his, even if it wasn't for keeps. She guessed it stemmed from his background, from the things he had had to go without—the care, the love...

'Yes, we married for the sake of the baby,' he rasped. 'But that doesn't alter the fact that—whether you like it or not—we *are* still married, and that's how I intend it to stay.' Then, when she didn't respond, too stunned by his last remark, 'Look at me, Sanchia,' he commanded with menacing quietness. 'Look at me and smile.'

She managed one of those things at least, gazing up into his hard-boned face, at the mirthless curve of his mouth and the glacial quality of his eyes. And she realised that she had thoroughly underestimated him. He hadn't tried to retrieve her memory to appease his conscience when it came to divorcing her. She was his wife and he was determined to keep it that way, whether out of pride or simple commitment or duty. *Duty is the code by which Alex Sabre lives*. And now he wanted everyone—including his ex-fiancée—to think that everything was hunky-dory, to think that everything was right! Because pride wouldn't let him admit to anyone that his marriage had failed!

'Don't look so belligerent,' he advised smoothly. 'If we were back home now, and I started peeling off your clothes, you wouldn't be objecting. In fact it wouldn't take very much before you were begging me to make love to you.'

'Shut up!' she hissed, with a furtive glance over his shoulder in case anyone overheard him.

'Why? Don't you want them to know that my wife can't get enough of her husband's attentions? Perhaps we should shout it to the world.'

'Don't!' As he made to turn, looking every bit as if he would carry out his threat, she clutched desperately at the sleeve of his jacket. There was something driving him tonight, and right at that moment she didn't think she could put anything past him.

'Why not?' His face was all light and flitting shadows, created by the lamps that hung amongst the numerous ornamental trees. 'Ashamed of it?'

'No, just degraded,' she admitted desolately.

'Degraded?' From the quick gesture of his mouth she had hit him where it hurt—at the core of his ego.

'Entirely,' she said through clenched teeth, wanting to hurt him as he was hurting her.

'Don't be,' he advised, recovering, his response hard and clipped. 'A woman isn't expected to love a man these days to get the same amount of pleasure from sex as he does. But then we already know that—don't we, darling? Have known it from that very first night.'

Sanchia's eyes fell, embarrassed, to the dark red of her nails, lying against the white fabric that tamed his impressive shoulders. 'I don't want to talk about that.'

'I'll bet you don't!' His sarcasm was unyielding. 'Well, let's not talk. Let's act!'

Taking her by surprise, he caught her so close to him that she was forced to arch her back against his arm before his mouth descended masterfully over hers.

His kiss was hard and demonstrative, and it took all her will-power just to stand there and take it—which he knew she would do rather than cause a scene. She could feel his angry arousal, and even in spite of that found herself responding shamelessly to it.

Bright wings of colour flamed across her cheeks, and her breasts were straining against the smooth bodice of her dress when he eventually lifted his head.

'I don't want to sleep with you tonight.'

He grimaced. 'That's good. Because the last thing on my mind, Sanchia, is sleeping.'

'I'm serious!'

'So am I.'

Out of the corner of her eye she saw the young Croft woman slip inside the marquee, recognised the defeat on her pinched and ravaged features.

'I hate you,' she said softly, only because she couldn't bear to acknowledge the effect he was having on her even while he was hurting her like this.

'We've already established that. You've said it so much, Sanchia, you really don't need to convince me any more.'

'Then let me go.'

His hair gleamed darkly under the lights as he tilted his head to gaze down at her. 'Am I holding you against your will?' His voice held nothing but derision. 'It's sex holding you here, darling. Nothing else. You admitted as much yourself, only a couple of days ago.'

Only because she hadn't wanted him to guess how much she cared when she had so recklessly seduced him that morning! she remembered, tortured. 'That's all it ever was!' Then, in one desperate bid to free herself from the emotional chains that bound her to him, she blurted out, 'I married you for the sake of my baby, not for any other reason, Alex. Why can't you accept that? Accept that this is one thing Luke had that you never will?'

The music had stopped. People were applauding. The duo were taking a break. Around them the other dancers were milling about, chatting, laughing, oblivious to the tortured girl and the blenched features of the man staring down at her, both motionless, as though they were carved out of stone.

'If that's the way it is,' he said eventually, slipping a hand into his trouser pocket, 'there's a flight leaving for the UK tomorrow night. I'm sure you'll be more than pleased to know you're perfectly at liberty to take it.'

The cool delivery of those words devastated her. Something that felt like a ton weight seemed to be pressing down on her chest. 'You really mean that? You won't try and stop me?'

He was looking at her askance, those grey eyes hard, stripping her raw. 'It's what you want, isn't it?'

No! her heart cried miserably, and as she realised she had said too much—wished she could retract it. But those inexorable features had never looked colder or more austere, and dully she answered, 'Yes.'

Someone passed, acknowledging him. He dipped his head, his smile perfunctory. Still the urbane guest, the sophisticated advocate, summoning all the right responses—ruthless, unaffected, inmovable—while she felt as though the universe were crumbling around her, felt herself crumbling with it as he stated decisively, 'Then leave it to me.'

He didn't sleep with her that night, as he had threatened to, and he was already out the next morning when she came downstairs, late and bleary-eyed, the dark hollows above her cheeks testimony to the hours she had lain awake, crying deep into her pillow.

'I'm out most of tomorrow,' Alex had stated when they had arrived back the previous night, after a journey when neither of them had spoken a word. 'I will, however, be in to take you to the airport later. See you safely off,' he had added, as though in doing so he would be executing one final act of duty.

'Don't bother!' she had snapped back, and when he had tried to insist she had added, 'I really don't want you there!'

He had looked grim, but she had got her point across, she realized. He hadn't suggested it again. He probably thought her as hard and uncaring as he was, but in truth she didn't think she could have survived saying goodbye to him at the airport.

She spent a couple of hours packing, and popped out around mid-afternoon to fetch a couple of things from the nearest general store, hoping the long walk would help to make her feel better.

A first-class, single air ticket was on the dressing table when she got back.

So she had missed him, and he obviously wasn't coming back, she realised, picking it up. All the good the walk had done her was wasted as she struggled with her tears, taking no comfort from telling herself that it was all her own fault for convincing him that that was what she wanted.

He had left something else too.

Frowning, she reached for the fine gold chain he had draped over her box of cosmetic tissues with its little bird attached—the one he had given her the night she had had that dream. There was a note beside the tissues, with just five words written upon it.

I would have thee gone...

Pain speared her to the heart. It was a quote from *Romeo and Juliet*. There was more to that piece of prose, something about a bird, but she couldn't remember it and he hadn't completed it.

With tears burning her eyes, something sprang into her brain—a fragment of memory she hadn't until now retrieved.

He had recited the whole piece to her the day he had placed that chain around her neck, and she had laughed up at him over her shoulder for quoting Shakespeare. But it hadn't been the other night. It had been during that glorious two weeks they had spent here together before they were married. Instinctively she knew that it was the same pendant. The one he had bought for her after she'd got upset in the restaurant that first time over a lobster. An apology for hurting her sensibilities. That was how he'd put it.

'Birds and fishes—they're both sacrosanct to you, aren't they?' he'd remarked gently as he'd finished fastening the chain, and then he'd kissed her, and it had been at that moment that she'd secretly acknowledged how much she loved him.

It had been like a double mockery of her foolish love for him when she'd lost that pendant, the same day she'd discovered she was losing her baby.

A sob was wrenched from her now as she looked down again at the part of the quotation he had so carefully selected. *I would have thee gone…*

He couldn't have put it any more clearly if he'd tried!

It was late afternoon when she rang Hilary to tell her she was leaving. 'So soon?' the woman remarked, having already been informed about Sanchia regaining her memory. 'So he didn't get all his own way?'

'What?' Sanchia queried, frowning, but Hilary had already changed the subject.

'Sanchia, wait!' she urged, just as Sanchia was thanking her for all her kindness. 'You've got a couple of hours before you're due at the airport. Let's meet for a coffee. Say in…twenty minutes?'

'I can't help feeling you're making a big mistake,' Hilary told her over a cappuccino outside a small waterside café, under the shade of a pink and white sun umbrella.

'Maybe, but I can't stay here—and I certainly can't stay married to him,' Sanchia told her unhappily. 'It isn't fair to either of us. He wouldn't have married me if I hadn't been having his baby. You do know that, don't you?'

'Wouldn't he?'

Sanchia frowned at this woman with her no-nonsense manner and her twinkling blue eyes. She sounded so decided, so sure.

'You don't have to smooth things over for me just to try and make me feel better,' Sanchia advised sadly, adding cream to her espresso. She felt she needed something strong to keep her going. 'Anyway, what other reason would he have had?'

'Only that he loves you.'

Sanchia almost laughed. She hadn't put Hilary down as a romantic. 'Oh, he's tried! I'll grant him that.'

'Tried?' Hilary gave her one of those challenging looks from under her deep brows that Sanchia had only ever seen her use on Alex. 'If you think that, then I don't think you know your husband as well as you think you do.'

'Oh?' Sanchia prompted, feeling oddly castigated, her eyes trained on the fluttering white fringes of the sun umbrella.

'He said you met here on the island—and that he let you go before he could find out your name.'

Behind her dark glasses, Sanchia could feel herself flushing scarlet. Since the storms the intense heat had eased back a little, and a hint of a breeze was drifting in off the shimmering ocean.

'He didn't give me any details other than about the way you looked,' Hilary assured her, although Sanchia knew the psychiatrist would have sussed the situation—knew she had when her mouth tilted and gave an odd little quirk when she said, 'Poor Alex. I don't think any woman ever ran out on him in his life. He wanted to know if I knew who you were or where you might have come from. He didn't confide much in me, but I knew he was determined to find you—and I think he darn near turned himself inside out trying to do just that.'

A small spark lit Sanchia's eyes. 'He did?' Was Hilary serious? 'But when I saw him again…' Her words tailed off, her brow furrowing.

'He'd found out you'd been his brother's fiancée, with all the implications that carried with it,' Hilary supplied. 'I know. He did tell me that much.'

'And did he tell you that he was engaged to Yasmin Croft as well?' Sanchia chipped in, hurting. 'And that he would have married her if he hadn't felt it his duty to marry me?'

Something exploded from Hilary that sounded remarkably like, 'Tosh!' And then, after a moment, 'That girl's been after him since she first left school, according to her long-suffering brother. And I gather Alex probably indulged her to a degree because she was his friend's kid sister. I understand she's very accomplished artistically, but also very jealous and very imaginative too. If there's ever been any suggestion that she was going to marry Alex, then she spread those rumours around herself. The Croft women believe in pulling out all the stops to get what they want—whether it be a bigger and better house, a rip-roaring party or, in Yasmin's case, Alex Sabre. But not a chance in hell. He loves you,' Hilary repeated.

Sanchia's expression was guarded. 'He hasn't told you so.'

'He doesn't have to—and nor would he,' the psychiatrist stated bluntly. 'That man's got more pride than the Serengeti's got lions, and he isn't likely to tell you, either, or even admit it to himself if you don't meet him halfway. I wasn't sure that I approved of his withholding the facts from you, but I think it was because he wanted you to get to know him for who he is, and not the man you thought you married. From what I can gather you were hurt very badly by his brother, Sanchia. But Alex isn't going to do what Luke did. He's a different type of man altogether.'

'So are you're saying I'm to blame?'

'Partly,' Hilary stated candidly. 'But Alex too, for being so proud and so damnably stubborn. Stand up to him. Fight with him. But for goodness' sake, Sanchia, don't leave him like this!

He's lost a lot too, you know. The mother he was so close to. His father and brother. His unborn child. Don't put the last spoke in by making him lose his marriage as well.'

In the taxi back to the house, Sanchia mulled over everything Hilary Tuxford had said. Was the psychiatrist right? she wondered, wanting yet scarcely daring to believe that Alex Sabre might actually be in love with her. He had never told her so. In fact he had done very little to try and alleviate her doubts and suspicions. But then, neither had she told him of *her* feelings, and, as he had stated quite bluntly the previous night, a woman wasn't always in love with a man just because she was willing to go to bed with him. And where her own sexual history with him was concerned he had—or thought he had—every proof!

Then there was that very incriminating quotation he had left on the dressing table under her pendant. *I would have thee gone...*

Could he really have been cruel enough to have written that? Or were those three little dots supposed to jolt her into remembering something which, exasperatingly, she still couldn't bring to mind?

Nevertheless, the things Hilary had told her had given her at least a gram of hope. Made her think about things she wouldn't even have considered before. Was her marriage to Alex worth trying to save? Was it worth the risk of humiliating herself if she stayed only to be told he didn't want her?

That last thought made her shudder, but she loved him too much, she acknowledged, to let her doubts and anxieties get in the way of what was, after all, a matter of life and if not exactly death then certainly a lonely, empty existence without him.

With tears streaming down her face at the knowledge that it was worth any risk at all if there was even the slimmest chance that her husband might be in love with her, she paid off the taxi, let herself into the house, and decided right there and then what she was going to do.

CHAPTER TWELVE

HE WAS sitting at the bar, looking straight ahead at the picture that dominated one wall of the elegant cocktail lounge—the lounge beneath the ballroom where in another lifetime, it seemed to Sanchia, that impressive ice sculpture had stood.

It was the picture, she remembered without any hesitation, that he had shown her in that restaurant back in London, which had made her react with such panic. Because, of course, *she* had taken the original photos, superimposing the real swan on top of its frozen counterpart. The magnificent cob breaking out of the sculpture, coming from within itself—just as she had done, out of the darkness, out of the void.

Alex had once said that it bore the hallmark of her genius— which was a bit over the top, she'd thought at the time. She had called it *Out of the Darkness*, unaware of how aptly it would apply to the cruel blow life was to deal her in robbing her of her memory, and she had won a competition with it before donating it to this hotel when Alex had brought her back here with him to attend a charity function during that first holiday. She had been so in awe of him, yet pregnant with his baby and already half-way to being desperately in love.

His dark head lowered now as he picked up the whisky glass in front of him, drained it of its contents and set it down on the bar again. Although he'd offered to see her off tonight, she knew he'd had a meeting here. Alone now, his meeting concluded, he looked stupendous in a dark business suit that accentuated his dynamic presence. Handsome. Charismatic. Darkly aloof.

Perhaps he wouldn't welcome seeing her, she thought with a queasy feeling in her stomach. He thought she was on a plane for the UK, that she'd be somewhere over the Atlantic by now. Perhaps she had already left it too late.

Tentatively, her pulse accelerating, she moved across the lounge on legs that felt decidedly wobbly, taking a deep breath as she came up behind him, because he still didn't know she was there, and it took every ounce of courage she possessed to whisper, 'Can I get you another drink?'

The muscles beneath the elegant cut of his jacket flexed, stiffening his broad back, and a little of Sanchia's already stretched nerve deserted her when he didn't even turn around.

'What am I supposed to say to that, Sanchia?' he intoned, without looking at her. 'Very probably? But then I suppose there's very little you *couldn't* do—especially to a man's dignity and self-respect.'

Against the subdued atmosphere of their surroundings his words were hard and flaying. But the similarity of the scenario egged her on regardless. She was not lost in the darkness now, but drawing on clear, keen recollection for every carefully chosen syllable. 'Then perhaps I ought to rephrase that? *May* I get you a drink?'

He swung round on his stool then, those intelligent eyes derisive as they acknowledged the situation, taking in her white silk crop top and matching silk trousers, her clear complexion, pouting red lips and long, loose ebony hair. 'Better.' His incredibly direct gaze made hers falter, bringing it involuntarily to the expensive fabric straining across his hard muscled thighs. 'But the answer's still thanks, but no thanks.'

It was like a parody of that other time, only with roles reversed. She the pursuer—hungry, persistent, presumptuous; he the pursued—hard-hitting, aggressive, unapproachable. Yet just as before she couldn't help but feel he was still the one calling the shots.

'Too complicated?' she whispered, remembering. If he wanted to continue playing this game with her, she thought achingly, then she could do it—couldn't she?

'Much too complicated.' The squaring of those broad shoulders seemed to underscore it, a hard, impervious wall she couldn't scale.

'Really?' Sanchia's voice cracked. This wasn't going at all as she had planned. 'I was under the impression you'd welcome seeing me here.'

'Were you?' His laugh was soft and mirthless. 'And, if I'm not mistaken, isn't this where you ask me if I'm married?'

'Alex, don't…'

'Why not? Too much a replay of the first time? I thought that was what you wanted. Well, since we seem to be on that roller-coaster, then the answer to that last question is, I think: not any more.'

An arrow of pain shot through her, so sharp it almost lanced the breath from her airways. 'Alex, please…'

'Shh.' The sudden warmth and pressure of his long fingers on her mouth was enervating, paralysing her with its sensuality, leaving only her nostrils alive to the achingly familiar scent of his aftershave that still clung to his hand. 'You don't know my name, remember?' Those powerful thighs splayed and closed again, trapping her inside them, kick-starting every impulse into throbbing life while those sensual fingers moved to burn a caressing path along her jaw. 'Ironic, isn't it, darling, what infinite pleasure there is to be had in anonymity?'

'Alex, don't.' Her heart was beating so fast she could hardly speak.

'Why not?' His voice was the voice of a man hardened by cynicism, lethally evocative over the soft piped music playing behind the bar. 'Isn't that why you're here?'

Turning her head from that caressing hand, Sanchia pulled herself forcibly out of his sensually disturbing grip. 'No.'

'Then I'm sorry, darling…' he was uncoiling himself from the stool, extracting a couple of notes from his wallet '…because I'm afraid it's all I've got.'

'That's not true,' Sanchia argued, swallowing from the impact of his dominating height and build as he towered above her, his masculinity exciting her even through her desperation—as it always had. 'You tried to show me—tell me—and I wouldn't listen.'

For a moment, when he glanced down at her, she could see a whole gamut of emotions beneath the hard austerity of his face. But then he turned away, saying as he tossed the notes down onto the bar, 'Forget it, sweetheart. It's all we ever had.'

'No, it isn't—' She clammed up as the Bermudian barman moved towards them to pick up his tip. He thanked Alex and wished them both a pleasant evening. He knew them. Of course he did. Although they had stayed in a smaller hotel last time, Alex represented the owner here—which was why he had obviously been careful not to bring her here before.

'You were staring at my swan picture.' She looked up into his face as he stood there, waiting for her to precede him out of the lounge. 'Why?'

'What do you want to hear me say, Sanchia?' Silently he urged her on and she walked ahead of him, ignoring the interested looks she could feel they were drawing from all sides. 'That it cut me to the core—remembering when and where you took it? Do you want to drag me to my knees? Is that it?'

She glanced up at him as they came through the open archway into the reception area, her heart aching, acutely aware of his close proximity and the raw animal magnetism that was attracting the interest of every woman who happened to pass. 'Could anyone ever do that?' she asked sadly.

'If you want the truth,' he told her, stopping in the bright and busy plant-decked area of the vestibule, 'I was thinking how paradoxical it all was.'

A small pained line creased Sanchia's velvety brows. 'Paradoxical?'

'It's called *Out of the Darkness*.' As if she needed reminding! 'It just made me wonder why you could only accept me while your mind was totally locked—devoid of all knowledge of who I was—both this time and the first time. Why you couldn't just shrug off your prejudices, grow up, and accept things for what they are, instead of what you imagine them to be.'

It all sounded so final, and she looked at him quickly, her heart bursting to breaking point.

I'm ready to now!

Every feminine cell screamed it at him and yet she still couldn't say it—only with her eyes, dark with all the agony of her hopeless love for him.

'I found the note you left with my pendant.' He was walking on again, and she had to hurry to keep up. 'It was *my* pendant, wasn't it?'

He didn't even need to acknowledge it.

'Where did you find it?'

'What does it matter now?' He was striding on, grim-faced. 'Except that you've got it back?'

'And the rest of that quotation.' She had a job keeping her voice steady after the ominous dismissal in what he had just said. *What does it matter now*? 'You wanted me to remember it, didn't you?'

He had slowed his pace, his big body taut, his mouth set hard, inexorable. Because of course she had remembered it at last, and the words flowed out of her before she could even stop them. '"I would have thee gone; And yet no further than a wanton's bird, Who lets it hop a little from her hand…"'

Her voice was trembling as she finished. Because surely if he had wanted her to remember that it meant he wanted her with him? Didn't it?

He hadn't moved, his face inscrutable, and now, with coolly measured movements, he consulted the gold watch with its black strap that lay against the dark hairs of his wrist, remarking incisively, 'Shouldn't you be on a plane?'

His indifference speared her, slicing across her raw emotions with such cruelty that she nearly doubled up.

How could he? And how could she even have imagined that he would soften towards her? Let herself hope and believe that all she had imagined and all that Hilary had said was true? She had been a fool, and she had allowed herself to be humiliated because of it. All the time her instincts had been wrong, and Hilary had been terribly mistaken. Alex Sabre didn't love her at all!

'Thanks for reminding me!' It was a pained castigation, torn out of her by her humiliation and her wretchedness. 'It just so happens I've missed it! I missed it because I couldn't just go home and part from you on such unfriendly terms!' Hot tears she could no longer contain were glistening in her eyes, and her voice was rising with each pained, frustrated syllable. 'I rang up and cancelled the flight! But don't worry. I'll pay you back! I'd hate you to be out of pocket for a flight I didn't take just because I was careless enough to miss it! Just because I was stupid enough to think you'd want me to come back as much as I wanted to come back to you!'

She hadn't realised how many people were suddenly milling around the vestibule. An influx of guests returning from the island's hotspots; late diners waiting for taxis; people summoning lifts. She saw only Alex's unreadable face, saw his mouth take on a sardonic curve, and she would have turned away, unable to bear it, if he hadn't grabbed her wrist and stopped her, saying with soft, devastating purpose, 'Then let's not let all your efforts be wasted, shall we?'

His words had barely registered when she felt one arm go around her back, the other under her knees. She couldn't believe it! He was actually lifting her off her feet!

'What are you doing...?' People were watching them. Mortified, Sanchia glimpsed their amused faces and tore her gaze quickly away. Even more mortifyingly she heard someone close to them start to clap, and then the whole reception area was suddenly echoing with raucous applause. 'Put me down! People are watching!' Kicking out, she landed him a whack on his side which made such little impression on that hard torso she might have saved herself the effort. 'Put me down, for goodness' sake! What will people think?'

'Perhaps they'll realise what you clearly haven't. That your husband's taking you somewhere where he's going to ravage you until you're sick of the sight and taste and feel of him. Or at the very least until you're pregnant. And stop kicking me,' he advised dryly. 'You'll just draw attention to yourself!'

Draw attention to herself!

A small bubble of hysteria rose up in her throat as he shouldered his way into a lift that had just pinged open. An elderly couple, stepping out, looked at them as they passed. Sanchia buried her face against the spicy heat of his throat so that she wouldn't have to see their knowing smiles, her body tingling from the heat of those strong hands through the fine silk of her top and trousers, her mind reeling with what he had just said.

Until you're pregnant...

'You can't do this to me,' she sobbed, when the doors had whined closed behind them. Mercifully, they were the only ones in the lift.

'Can't I?'

'Not when I've made up my mind to leave you.'

'Especially as you've made up your mind to leave me.'

'Don't I get any say?'

'Only in the way you say it best.'

'No, Alex...' She fought him with all her ineffectual strength. 'This isn't fair!'

'Everything's fair in love and war,' he reminded her, unrelenting. 'As far as I see it, I shall just have to keep whittling down your resistance until you tell me the truth.'

'The truth about what?'

'About how much you love me.'

'No, I don't! I hate you.' But she said it without any conviction at all.

His strong teeth showed white as he laughed at her feeble attempt to convince him. 'Just the flipside of the same coin, darling.'

'You don't love *me*.' How could he if he could make her suffer like this?

'But you came back regardless.'

Yes, she had, she thought despairingly, realising he had just confirmed it. So just how much respect did that mean she had for herself?

'No, Alex, please! Not the penthouse suite,' she protested softly, her brows pleating as he stepped with her into the softly lit corridor. Not there. Not where they had made love without words or feeling. Not where she had conceived...

He smiled, but there was a strange inflexion in his voice as he said, 'Do you think I'm entirely insensitive?'

'Yes. Because if you weren't you'd tell me why you're doing this.'

He was slipping his key into a lock. 'Because I like making love with you.'

'And?'

A door sprang open. 'Because I can't get enough of you.'

'And?'

'Isn't that enough?'

'No,' she breathed hopelessly. 'Can't you see? I can't keep doing this with you if you're only staying with me just because you made a commitment. I would have forgiven you anything, wouldn't have cared if you'd had a thousand mistresses, if you'd just told me once that you loved me.'

'No, you wouldn't,' he countered. 'You couldn't have lived with that. No one could if they were truthful with themselves.' The door was kicked shut behind him. 'But maybe I'll just have to tell you a thousand times—as well as admit that I don't even have one mistress.'

A thousand times? What was he saying? Her heart did a double somersault. That he was in love with her? 'But you—' Her arms around his neck, she broke off, her amber eyes puzzled, still suspicious. 'Hilary said you hadn't—'

'Hilary?'

Of course. He didn't know about that. 'I wanted to believe it,' she went on, deciding that confessing her little chat with the psychiatrist could wait until another time. 'But if it's true why did Yasmin say you discussed marriage with *her*?'

'Because I did,' he admitted matter-of-factly, bearing her effortlessly across the bedroom. And when Sanchia sat up, looking at him with wide, anguished eyes, he merely laughed softly at her tortured suspicion. 'A very long discussion—to make her realise once and for all that I *was* married and intended to *stay* married to you. Why are you always so ready to take her word over mine?' he enquired, in a voice that was strangely hoarse, and he dropped down with her onto the yielding double bed, cradling her there on his lap. 'Is it because of Luke? Because of what he did to you?'

It was strange, she thought, that he should have decided that, when Hilary had suggested exactly the same thing to her. So perhaps it was true. She had been so hurt by what Luke had done it would have been difficult trusting any man again, let alone one who seemed so far out of her reach emotionally and whom she wanted so much...

'You seemed to spend so much time working late during our marriage, and even since we've been back here there have been times when you went out at night without me.'

'Only because I didn't know any other way of keeping my hands off you. What I really wanted to do from the start was tell you who I was, take you back to the apartment and resume our lives together. But I didn't want to do anything that would drive you away from me again.' His deep voice shook with an intensity of emotion. 'So I decided to bring you here. At least we'd been happy together here, and I could take my time with you—not rush anything or plunge you straight into being with people who'd known you. The purchase of my house here wasn't finalised until after you'd left.'

That was what he'd started to tell her over dinner that first night they'd arrived, Sanchia remembered. Except that he'd stopped himself in time...

'I didn't realise until I saw Danny.' Beneath the immaculate suit his deep chest lifted heavily. 'Yasmin had come over with him too. I couldn't believe fate could do that to me when she'd contributed towards all your absurd conjectures in the first place.'

'I thought it was her you really wanted to be married to,' Sanchia whispered, running her fingers over the smooth cloth of his lapel. 'I thought that was what you meant when you said that if you were honest, I wouldn't thank you for it. That you weren't telling me we were married because you intended to get a divorce.'

'I've never wanted a divorce,' he murmured thickly. 'Not now. Not before. Even if I wasn't understanding enough towards you during our marriage. And I stayed away from you so much because plunging myself into my work seemed the only way of keeping myself sane. I wanted to love you so much, but you seemed determined to put up barriers between us. I know now that it was only because you'd been so badly hurt by a double dose of deceit. First Luke's and then Yasmin's. I could quite happily throttle her,' he said savagely, with hard lines scoring his strong, handsome face.

The depth of his angry feeling brought Sanchia's hand up to cup his cheek, soft fingers stroking over the rough texture of his jaw.

'I wouldn't have believed any of the things she said if you'd just told me the things I needed to hear. But you never did—not in so many words anyway. You're so clever with them, and you use them to such devastating effect in the courtroom. Why not try using just a few of them on me?'

'All right,' he said. 'If that's what you want.' His tension easing, he laughed softly, pressing his lips against the scented softness of her hair. 'Is your real name Sanchia Sabre?' She murmured her smiling agreement. It sounded so good to hear him say it. 'Then why couldn't you take that as proof of the part I wanted you to play in my life?'

'I wanted to,' she admitted. 'But things kept happening to make me doubt it. I was pregnant…and I just couldn't believe you would have wanted to marry me for any other reason.'

'Any more than I could make myself believe *you* weren't marrying *me* solely for the same reason. And when you confessed as much that last night, on the terrace at the Crofts' place…'

'I was just hurting so much,' Sanchia murmured, not wanting to remember. Purposefully her hand slid down, tugged gently at the impeccable knot of his tie.

'When you lost the baby, you thought I didn't understand what you were going through…' His deep voice trembled against the shining silk of her hair. 'But I was just as cut up about it as you were.'

'I felt so lonely—isolated,' she admitted, her breath catching as she remembered the pain of it. 'And you didn't seem to want me around.'

'I know. I was hurting too much. We both were. But I thought I'd lost you then—that it was pointless even trying any more. I needed a shock to jolt me out of my stupidity, and your leaving me as you did gave me the biggest shock of my life. You don't know how long and hard I looked for you before I found you in Scotland. And then when I called round to those crummy little lodgings you were staying in to bring you back that day and you'd gone…'

She could feel the way the muscles bunched in his broad back as he, too, relived the pointless misery of that time.

'I thought I was never to know a worse agony—until I received that letter from your solicitor. I knew it was finally over then—that there was no point in pursuing you any further. That I shouldn't have bamboozled you into marrying me, and that you were never going to come back. If I hadn't thought like that I'd have carried on looking for you, and then I would have known about your accident—your amnesia. My poor love, you were suffering and I didn't even know about it. Can you possibly imagine how that's made me feel?'

'I'm sorry,' she murmured. 'I didn't want to send that letter.

And the only reason I stepped off that pavement and into that car was because I was crying so much over what I'd done.'

'But you were so determined to leave me—resist me!' he exclaimed, with incredulity darkening the steel-grey of his eyes. 'When I found you in Scotland you acted as though I were no better than a jailer who had come to drag you back to a prison you couldn't stand. How could I possibly have known?'

'If you'd let me know how *you* felt, I would have told you just how much I loved you,' Sanchia said with tears in her eyes. 'We've wasted so much time, haven't we?'

'Yes.' And then, 'Tell me now,' he commanded softly.

'I love you.'

She couldn't say anything else, because his arms had tightened around her and his mouth was covering hers in a way that told her she could protest all she liked—this time he never intended to let her go.

Their passion swallowed them up. A storm of emotions that left in its wake a scattering of hastily discarded clothes and painful misunderstandings. It was like a mutual and long-awaited homecoming that left them lying contented together, warm and satiated and sleepy.

Much later, Alex said, 'I dreamt you'd gone. I was lying here alone because I couldn't bear to go back to an empty house.'

Sanchia raised herself up from the crook of his arm, her hair tumbling against the dark velvet of his shoulder. In his eyes she read the pain that losing her would mean to him, knew that that was the only reason this room had been so conveniently to hand.

'Do you love me that much?' she whispered.

Dark lashes veiled Alex's eyes before he gazed down into hers. Her warmth against him was all the reassurance he needed.

'No, much more than that,' he breathed, stroking her hair, inhaling her perfume and the musky scent of their loving. 'I don't deserve you,' he murmured. 'Not after the way I practically threatened you into marrying me.'

'You were rather intimidating.' A wave of desire rippled

through her as she returned his lazy smile, pressing against the warm hand that was caressing her cheek.

Catching his fingers in hers, she surveyed their linked hands, frowning as she turned his over. 'How did you do this?' Gently she bent to touch her tongue to the thin red lines that still scarred his lean, dark hand.

'Fighting everything that was keeping you from me.'

He meant it, she realised, her love for him so strong she felt as though something were squeezing at her heart.

'I love you,' she whispered, because nothing else would do.

Those strong fingers tightened almost painfully around hers. 'So what made you do something so crazy? When did you fall in love with me, Sanchia?'

'I think,' she said, pretending to consider, 'it was downstairs. The first time I looked at you through my viewfinder.'

Those grey eyes widened in disbelief. 'But you were still in love with Luke.'

'I thought I was,' she confessed. 'But I've known for a long time that I was never in love with him. Not in the way I love you. He just didn't affect me the way you did—do! Right from the very beginning I couldn't help myself with you.'

That firm male mouth moved wryly. 'I'd noticed,' he drawled, catching her other hand before she could deliver a playful thump to his shoulder. 'Do you know the penalty for assaulting a barrister of the High Court?'

She gave a delicious little shiver. 'Does it carry a life sentence, m'lud?'

He slid his fingers along her slender back, felt her body tauten in anticipation.

'Most definitely,' he decided firmly, hardening from the excitement he could feel rising in her, his senses sharpening at the slick warmth of her as she wedged her thigh between his, at the tantalising silk of her hair as it fell against his chest, the sultry perfume of her skin.

'And do I get any time off for good behaviour?' Her tongue

was trailing down his chest now, moving over his body with hot little darting movements that were threatening to drive him insane.

'Definitely not,' he rasped, his powerful chest lifting in the heat of his barely constrained desire as her moist mouth continued to play havoc with his senses. 'The better you behave, the longer I'm keeping you under lock and key!'

'Mmm,' Sanchia murmured, delighting in having such exquisite power over such a proud and powerful man. 'In that case, I'll come quietly, m'lud.'

'Not if I've got anything to do with it,' he groaned, rolling her over. And, with his mouth coming down on hers, proceeded to show her what he meant.

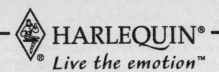

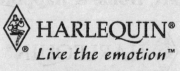

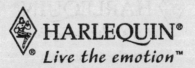

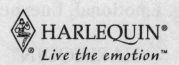

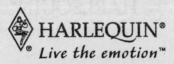

Harlequin® Historical
Historical Romantic Adventure!

Imagine a time of chivalrous knights and unconventional ladies, roguish rakes and impetuous heiresses, rugged cowboys and spirited frontierswomen— these rich and vivid tales will capture your imagination!

Harlequin Historical... they're too good to miss!

HHDIR06

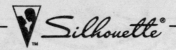

SPECIAL EDITION™

Emotional, compelling stories that capture the intensity of living, loving and creating a family in today's world.

Modern, passionate reads that are powerful and provocative.

nocturne

Dramatic and sensual tales of paranormal romance.

Romances that are sparked by danger and fueled by passion.